'You're my m

'Yep.'

Davey nodded. 'Then I guess it's OK to tell you my name,' he decided gravely. 'I'm David Campbell Inger and I'm four.'

David Campbell Inger. Aged four. Button-nosed, freckled—and a tiny, younger version of the man kneeling beside him. There were some facts that couldn't be denied.

'Lilly. . .' Hamish's voice held a note of stunned wonder. He looked down at Davey and it was like a man beholding a miracle.

'No!' Lilly said the word desperately. The questions would have to be answered, she knew—but not yet.

Marion Lennox has had a variety of careers—medical receptionist, computer programmer and teacher. Married, with two young children, she now lives in rural Victoria, Australia. Her wish for an occupation which would allow her to remain at home with her children and her dog led her to begin writing, and she has now published a number of medical romances.

Recent titles by the same author:

PRESCRIPTION—ONE BRIDE
PRESCRIPTION—ONE HUSBAND
BUSH DOCTOR'S BRIDE
A CHRISTMAS BLESSING

BRIDAL REMEDY

BY
MARION LENNOX

With thanks to Nicholas Hill for my car, and to all our
friends who make my research such a pleasure.

*MILLS & BOON, the Rose Device and
LOVE ON CALL are trademarks of the publisher.
Harlequin Mills & Boon Limited,
Eton House, 18-24 Paradise Road, Richmond, Surrey TW9 1SR*

© Marion Lennox 1996

ISBN 0 263 79997 2

*Set in Times 10 on 10¹/₂ pt. by
Rowland Phototypesetting Limited
Bury St Edmunds, Suffolk*

03-9612-51372

Made and printed in Great Britain

PROLOGUE

IT WAS a glorious day for a wedding.

The breeze sweeping the island was laden with the scent of eucalypts and the island's tiny chapel was packed to bursting. Most of Nooluk had turned out for this magic wedding of two of the island's three doctors.

For Hamish, this was a second wedding. At thirty-five, Dr Hamish Campbell was one of the most popular men on the island, his caring smile and other, more masculine attributes tempting the island's younger women—and some not so young—to insist that sore throats should be seen almost as soon as they tickled.

And Lilly—gentle, lovely Lilly with her delicious chuckle that surfaced at a moment's notice and her cloud of burnished curls—seemed every man's dream. A fairy-tale bride. . .

The hour had come. Only the tinkling of bellbirds in the branches high above the church broke the stillness. The church doors drew apart and every head turned to see.

Then the bellbirds were drowned out by the pure, triumphant notes of the 'Trumpet Voluntary'. Every man, woman and child drew in their breaths at the vision floating down the aisle—at Lilly moving slowly, mistily down the aisle toward her beloved Hamish.

Before her, proudly bearing two rings on a white velvet cushion, was Lilly's small son. Four-year-old Davey was perhaps the proudest person in church. He walked solemnly, carefully down the aisle before his mother's cloud of lace and satin and finally stepped aside to take the hand of the man who'd escorted Lilly down the aisle.

The man whose hand he took was Dr Angus McVie,

5

the island's third doctor. White-haired and halfway into his seventies, Angus smiled down at Davey—his soon-to-be great-nephew-by-marriage—and his wrinkled hand squeezed the trusting fingers of the child.

This was the answer to both their needs, the squeeze said. The joining of both their loved ones. . .

And then Angus McVie and four-year-old Davey stood silently together, man and child, to see Lilly and Hamish become one.

Some wish. . .

Angus McVie stared down at Lillian Inger's eyes smiling up at him from his nephew's photograph, and then he looked again at the letter in his hands. If only wishes were horses. . .

It was a beautiful wish. A truly magnificent wish. Angus closed his eyes, the memory of Hamish's past pain sweeping over him. Hamish was a nephew to be proud of. He was a fine young man and it was a tragedy for the lad to waste his life here, caring for his uncle and cutting himself off from the outside world.

And when he opened his eyes Angus knew what he must do.

Angus McVie had spent forty years treating the ills of the islanders—and this was one more ill that he was going to treat. . .

Angus had a heart problem. A bad one. His time left as a practising doctor was short and he knew it. What Angus was planning would need effort, and it would need courage. Did he have the courage?

The wedding was perfect. Perfect! Worth the risk? Who knew?

All Angus knew was that the cure for two lonely hearts was one wedding. All he had to do was make two stubborn hearts agree.

CHAPTER ONE

DR LILLY INGER sat in the bow of the ferry and held Davey as close as he'd tolerate. She was annoying her small son, she knew. Her arms were a protective circle more in line with Lilly's need for security than Davey's.

Four-year-old Davey's eyes were growing brighter the nearer they grew to the island. He'd been promised a new home, sunshine, beaches and swimming and he was close to bursting with excitement.

'Are we nearly there yet, Mummy? Is this land our island? Is our house on this side of the island? Can I see it from here? Mummy, how soon can we swim?'

Davey was almost bouncing with glee and if Lilly hadn't held him she suspected he'd be over the side to try and get there faster.

Lilly wasn't doing any anticipating. Not any more. Lilly was scared stiff.

She never should have agreed to this, she thought bleakly. She hadn't realised that the island was so— well, so isolated. Two miles from the mainland seemed like a tiny distance when she'd considered taking this job, but now. . .

She looked back at the receding coastline of Northern Australia and her uneasiness grew. In bad weather no one could get off the island. Maybe she should have stuck with her practice in the city.

Dr Angus McVie had been so convincing. Lilly thought back to her interview—or rather her consultation—last month and, despite her nerves, Lilly's mouth twisted into a rueful smile. Devious old scoundrel. . .

Angus McVie had booked into her Sydney surgery as a new patient, asking for a long consultation as he had a heart problem. When Lilly ushered him in she'd examined him with care and then he'd thrown her a job offer that was almost too good to refuse.

'We want a young female partner,' he'd growled. 'And we want you. We've heard you're a damned fine doctor—I can see that now for myself—and we've heard you're looking for a country practice. If we advertise the job on Nooluk we'll be swamped with applicants so we thought we'd do it the other way around. I asked the professor of general practice at your university if he could recommend someone with a bit of experience—and your name stood out.'

It had stood out because it had been the only name Angus had produced for the professor to comment on. In fact, Angus had written specifically to ask his friend to tell him all he knew about Lillian Inger, but Lilly wasn't to know that.

Lilly had been dumbstruck. 'But I couldn't. . .I can't. . .' She hesitated. 'Dr McVie, it's really nice of you to offer me the job, but. . .but I have a young child.' She bit her lip. 'Did the professor tell you I'm a single mother?'

'He did,' Angus McVie had beamed. 'And we have a housekeeper who loves children. We're two crusty widowers and one housekeeper in a house that can comfortably hold a score of people. Your rooms will be far enough from ours so a spot of kid's noise won't bother us—not that it would anyway. We have a swimming pool and a tennis court and the beach is a hundred yards down the track. All our rooms have a view of the sea. The practice isn't too demanding and it's a great lifestyle. Give us twelve months' trial and find out.'

'A house. . .and a housekeeper. . .'

'The house is attached to the surgery and our small four-bed clinic,' Angus had continued. 'Your little boy will be within calling distance of you all the time.'

Lilly had stared across at Angus in confusion. How had this elderly doctor known about Davey? Did he know instinctively how much Lilly hated leaving her little boy in child care?

'But. . .' Lilly had looked at this seemingly benign old doctor sitting on the other side of her consulting desk and she was thrown so much off balance that she found it hard to think of a sensible question. 'Dr McVie. . . It's a huge step. . .and to be presented with it so suddenly. . .' She swallowed. 'Maybe if I came to the island and met you and your partner. . .'

'My partner will like you as much as I do,' Angus beamed. His smile faded. 'I know this is a sudden offer. The professor tells me you've only been toying with the idea of a country practice and you'll need time to think, but he also tells me you've just been filling in here while one of the partners is overseas. It wouldn't hurt to give us a try. And I'm in a bit of a hurry, lass. With my heart problems I can't practise much. It's putting a strain on my partner and I'm worried about him.'

'Is he. . .?' Lilly bit her lip trying to figure how to ask without offending. 'Is your partner a similar age to you?'

'Good heavens, no.' Angus's face cleared. 'Are you worrying about being stuck with two old fogies? You needn't. There's only one dinosaur in the practice. I can give my partner a good few years, girl. There's heaps of work in the lad yet—though he looks older since he lost his wife.'

'And he's a general practitioner?'

'No.' Angus shook his head. 'He's a surgeon, though of course he does GP work as well. That's another reason you're attractive to us. You did a six-month anaesthetic internship, I gather, so you can give an anaesthetic in an emergency.' Angus rose then and smiled down at her.

'I've knocked you sideways, lass. I can see that. Look, here's a bundle of information about Nooluk. I'm in Sydney for a few days seeing specialists about my heart. If you're interested, ring me on this number and have a meal with me. But believe me, Dr Inger, you'll be missing out on the opportunity of a lifetime if you knock us back.'

An opportunity of a lifetime. . .

It had certainly seemed like that, Lilly thought as she hugged Davey tighter. On first impressions, the island of Nooluk was a magic place. . .

The ferry was pulling into a natural harbour. The sea was sapphire blue and Lilly could see schools of brilliantly coloured fish flashing by underneath the boat. From down here in the harbour the island seemed mostly bushland and mountains, though the brochures Lilly had studied in the past weeks said that there was a tourist resort and a tiny town nestled in the valley.

'We're here, Mummy! We're really, really here.' Despite the constriction of Lilly's arms, Davey managed three fast bounces. 'We're here on our very own island.'

Our very own island. . .

Lilly looked over the sparkling water to the beckoning land. Maybe it could be as good as Dr McVie had promised. Maybe it could. . .

For the first time, Lilly felt her host of misgivings give way to tingling anticipation. Dear heaven, let this work. She'd messed up so much else in her twenty-seven years. For once let her have made the right decision. . .

'My partner will probably meet the boat,' Angus McVie had told her when Lilly had phoned to make final arrangements. 'I'm not allowed to drive yet, thanks to overbearing specialists and their interfering orders, but I'll make sure he meets you. If you come over on a weekday there'll not be many on the ferry and if you have the bairn then my partner won't have trouble spotting you.'

Davey had been playing in the reception area when Angus had made his job offer, and Angus had touched

Davey's brilliant red hair with the beginnings of affection. 'There can't be many lads with hair like this—
and such black eyebrows! It's a charming combination,'
Angus had growled. 'And unusual.'

It was certainly unusual. Lilly had only ever seen the
combination once before. . .almost five long years ago
and never since. . .

There was no time for thoughts in that direction now.
The ferry was growing closer and closer to the island's
wharf and Davey had hauled himself from Lilly's clasp
and was tugging her hand in glee.

'We're here. We're here,' the child sang.

They had definitely arrived. Lilly looked over at the
wharf. So, who was meeting them? There was only one
man waiting. He must be. . .

And then Lilly's breath caught in her throat.

Red hair.

Red hair and dark, dark eyebrows. Brows that were
almost black. . .

Anticipation died in Lilly's heart as if it had never
been, pleasure fading in one swift stroke to be replaced
by absolute confusion.

Hamish Campbell. . . Hamish Campbell was here on
her lovely island—the island where she and Davey were
going to make a new life. An island that seemed to
have been conjured up by a good fairy.

No good fairy. Just Angus McVie. One conniving,
interfering old. . .

He couldn't have. . . Surely it had to be crazy coinci-
dence? Angus couldn't have engineered this—could
he? One despairing thought after another crashed into
Lilly's mind as she watched the figure of Hamish
Campbell come slowly into clearer focus.

There was no mistake. No one could mistake Hamish
Campbell for someone else.

Hamish was just as good-looking as ever, she thought
bitterly. Maybe a little older. The man had an ineffable
air of weariness about him that Lilly hadn't seen before

but he looked just as striking as she remembered. His tanned, muscled figure was leaning on a bollard watching the fish beneath the jetty with idle curiosity.

Tired or not, he looked somehow at peace. He looked at one with his world.

It was that same peaceful quality that had drawn Lilly to Hamish all those years ago. In the midst of her final, frenetic years of medical school, when all that seemed important were dry facts to be learned before exams, Hamish had taken her gently by the hand and taught Lilly that medicine was people. Medicine was listening and watching and caring. All the facts in the world meant nothing if a doctor wouldn't take the time to listen—take the time to see and take the time to care.

And for a while. . .for a few short weeks. . . Lilly had thought that he meant it. She had thought that Hamish Campbell was sincere and caring and loving and a really, really, special person—and she had loved him desperately for it.

Loved him so much that it had almost destroyed her life.

Dear heaven, had Angus McVie engineered this whole meeting out of some crazy thoughts of reconciliation? How could he fail to understand the misery this would cause?

Or maybe. . .or maybe Hamish had helped engineer it. Was this some dreadful extension of the hurt Hamish Campbell had caused her already?

She was mad to have come. It had been a risk to come here and the last time she'd taken a risk—the last time Lilly has thrown caution to the wind and followed her heart—it had ended in disaster.

That risk had been loving Hamish Campbell—and the worst part of it was that she still did.

Lilly stared across at the wharf and she looked at Hamish Campbell's hard, lean body leaning against the bollard with the ease of a man at one with his environment. She looked at his eyes shaded against a too strong sun, and her heart twisted with the same old lurch.

A heart that did nothing but betray her...

The men were tying the boat to the wharf now and Davey was hopping up and down on one leg in excitement. He was clinging to Lilly's sun-dress so hard that she feared it'd rip. She'd dressed with care, wanting to make a pretty, happy impression on two elderly widowers. Two elderly widowers... What a joke!

'Davey, I...I think I left my coat in the lounge,' Lilly said desperately. 'Could you go down and find it for me, please?'

Then, as Davey obligingly disappeared down into the cabin, Lilly turned to the ferry-master. The boat's engine had fallen silent, and the master had emerged from the wheelhouse to bid farewell to his passengers.

'Please... I've changed my mind,' Lilly told the boatman in a voice that was flat with despair. 'I'm not staying. I'm not even getting off the boat. How long before you leave?'

The ferry-master stared at Lilly with an expression of incomprehension. 'What the heck...?'

'How long before you leave?' Lilly repeated in a voice that was close to breaking with strain. 'I want to go back to the mainland.'

'But... Why?'

'I've just... I've just decided I've done the wrong thing.' In the corner of her eye Lilly saw Hamish speaking to one of the deckhands. The lad gestured toward Lilly and Lilly swept round fast so that only her back was facing Hamish. 'Please... There's someone here I don't want to meet. I don't want to get off the boat.'

'Who?' The captain gazed over Lilly's shoulder and his eyes lightened. 'The only man here is Doc Campbell. Hey, Doc...how's it going?' The ferry-master waved a cheery hand in greeting to Hamish, and to her horror Lilly heard feet jumping lightly onto the boat and treading toward them across the deck.

'Please. . . How long before you leave?' she demanded desperately, fighting down panic.

'I'm not.' The ferry-master had obviously decided that Lilly had flipped her lid and he wasn't in the mood for humouring her.

'N-not?'

'My home's on the island, Miss,' the boatman said flatly. 'I make one trip to the mainland every decent day and I make one trip back again. I've done both today so I'm finished. Now I'm off home to put my feet up. If you don't want to leave the boat I suggest you lock yourself in the cabin and stay there, but it's going to get mighty uncomfortable by morning. If you'll excuse me. . .'

And he stepped past her to meet Hamish.

Lilly bit her lip, her mind whirling. This was crazy. Impossible. . .

'Doc Campbell, what you doing at the wharf at this time of day?' the boatman demanded, ignoring Lilly completely as he greeted Hamish. Such foolishness, it seemed, deserved to be ignored and the ferry-master was obviously delighted to see the island's doctor. 'There's no broken legs or chickenpox down here,' he told him jovially. 'I can't even drum up a case of sea-sickness for you today.'

'That must be a first,' Hamish said drily in the voice Lilly knew so well. Maybe Hamish sounded older— there was certainly a trace of fatigue in his deep voice— but it was definitely the same Hamish. There was still the laughter.

With Hamish there had always seemed to be laughter just below the surface. It lurked at the ready, waiting for the ridiculous, and it was surfacing now. 'They tell me your master's ticket has ''Seafaring'' crossed out and ''Underwater Gymnastics'' pencilled in,' he teased the boatman.

'There's no need to get personal,' the ferry-master grinned. 'Just because I like a bit of rough weather. . .'

He hesitated and then turned uncertainly back to Lilly. His expression said that a doctor might be just what he needed with this tricky passenger. 'Now, miss. . .'

Lilly's mind was numb.

Her initial reaction was to do just what the boat captain suggested—bolt down into the cabin and stay there until morning—but what was that going to achieve? And how would she explain such crazy behaviour to Davey?

There was no choice. Like it or not, she was just going to have to grit her teeth and turn around. She had to face Hamish. Now. . .

One, two, three. . . Turn. . .

'Hamish,' she said, in a voice that sounded hopeless even to her. Flat with shock and sick to the marrow.

Hamish was still laughing, opening his mouth again to speak, but whatever he was about to say was cut off dead. His face froze into stunned incredulity as he slowly turned to stare at the girl before him.

'Lilly!'

It was a stunned whisper of stupefaction.

Shock was a real and solid thing as Lilly faced her ogre. The shock was so tangible that it was like a thick blanket, lowering over the boat and cutting off the outside world.

Silence. . . There was only the faint slap-slap of water against the hull. Nothing more.

Was it Lilly's imagination or did the whole world hold its breath? No one spoke. The boatman had heard the absolute shock in Hamish's voice, and the beefy ferry-master stood silently and stared.

Something was going on here that the boatman didn't understand, and the counsel of years told him that the best course in moments of incomprehension was to shut up and listen.

Both Hamish and Lilly had lost colour and Lilly looked like almost like she'd fall over.

The girl looked ill, the captain thought curiously.

Lilly's green eyes seemed too large for her pale face and her long, red-gold hair was making her face even paler. What the heck was she on about?

There was certainly something between these two, the boatman decided. Doc Campbell looked like he'd been slapped on the face with a wet fish. Or been dealt a body blow. . .

'What. . .what on earth are you doing here?' Hamish Campbell managed at last, and his normally deep, resonant voice seemed shaken to the core. He stood motionless on the boat-deck in the brilliant, tropical sunshine, the warm breeze ruffling his bright, wavy hair. Hamish was wearing light trousers and a short-sleeved shirt without a tie, and his clothes looked ruffled too. Dr Hamish Campbell looked ruffled to the bone.

He also looked exhausted.

He didn't look angry, though, the ferry-master decided. The girl looked like she'd been thrust into something against her will, but the doc looked as if he was seeing something out of a dream.

'Lilly,' Hamish said again and his voice was tinged with wonder. He stretched out a hand as if to touch some magic apparition but Lilly stepped back fast. It was as if Hamish's hand was searing hot she was so afraid of his touch.

'I. . .' Lilly tried hard to get her voice down from a squeak '. . .I think. . .there's been some crazy mistake. I'm here. . .I'm supposed to be meeting Dr Angus McVie. . . Not. . .not you.'

'You're our new partner?' Hamish's wide mouth twisted into a smile of stunned amazement. 'You. . . Lilly, I don't believe it.'

'You mean. . .' Lilly took a deep breath '. . .you mean. . .you mean you didn't engineer this? You and Angus?'

'Engineer. . .' Hamish shook his head as though there were too many thoughts for him to take on board all at once. 'Angus and I engineer. . .' His eyes narrowed against the sun and he stared at Lilly in incomprehension. 'I don't understand. How. . .?'

'Doc Campbell, is this the young lady you were expecting?' the ferry-master questioned. 'The new doctor?' He looked curiously at Lilly, clearly unhappy that this unhinged young woman was the island's latest medico.

'I suppose. . .I suppose she must be,' Hamish said slowly. 'Angus kept prevaricating on your name, Lilly. He could never remember—though he sure as anything remembered your qualifications. He said you were the best applicant by far for the job.'

'Maybe I was,' Lilly said bitterly. 'Out of a group of one.'

'But he said you answered his advertisement.' Hamish still had the struck-with-a-wet-fish look about him and his look of exhaustion stood out a mile. Whatever else was going on here on the island, Hamish Campbell was clearly not getting enough sleep.

'I didn't apply,' Lilly whispered. 'Dr McVie came and found me and offered me the job.'

'He found you and offered. . .' Hamish's eyes widened. 'But. . .'

'Look, I don't know why Dr McVie wanted me but. . .but I'm sorry, Hamish. Tell Dr McVie that he should have been honest. I can't stay here.'

Hamish's eyes crinkled in a sudden frown. Things were going on that he clearly didn't understand, but one thing was starting to stand out a mile. This woman was furious that he was here. 'Then. . .I assume you didn't know I was here?' he said flatly, pleasure draining fast.

'If I'd known you were here I never would have come,' Lucy told him and watched Hamish's tired face close. The warmth of his greeting dissipated to nothing. 'I thought you were old. . .I mean. . . Angus said that his partner was a widower.'

Hamish's closed look stayed. 'I am.'

Lilly's eyes flashed up to meet his then and there was no mistaking the pain behind Hamish's dark eyes. It made Lilly pause. For a moment—a fleeting instant—the anger faded enough to let compassion show.

'I'm sorry,' she said simply and she meant it. 'But, Hamish. . .' She bit her lip, pain searing through her as she searched for a course of action, and both men watched her with varying stages of wariness. 'This is impossible. Could I. . . Is there a hotel on the island? There's a resort here, isn't there? I'll stay at the resort until tomorrow and then I'll catch the boat back to the mainland.'

'The resort's at the other end of the island,' the captain said helpfully. 'I can give you a lift down there, miss.'

'You mean you're just turning tail and running?' Hamish demanded incredulously. 'After you've come all this way for the job?'

'That's just what I'm doing,' Lilly snapped. 'Do you think I'd stay here with you?'

Hamish's face had lost all expression. All pleasure at seeing her had gone completely. He ran a weary hand through his hair and shook his head.

'You've signed an agreement for a trial period.'

'It was signed under false pretences,' Lilly managed. 'You can't hold me to it.'

'I don't think I have a choice,' Hamish said grimly. His mind had been working fast. It didn't like what it was coming up with but the decision was unarguable. 'Are these your belongings, Lilly?'

Lilly looked down at the pile of luggage on the deck. Moving with a four-year-old was a nightmare. Davey had insisted that nothing should be left behind.

'Yes.'

'We've accommodation arranged at the house. Our housekeeper's expecting you.'

'I'm not staying with you,' Lilly said flatly.

Hamish closed his eyes. It seemed that he was fighting for control.

'Lilly, if I'd known. . .' His eyes flashed open again. 'I don't exactly want to stay with you either. Not if you feel as you obviously do. But I need you too much to tear up your contract. I'm sure Angus didn't tell you any lies when you agreed to come. He simply forbore to tell who his partner was. I doubt it'll hold up in court as an escape clause.'

'We'll let the lawyers decide that, shall we?'

'The lawyers aren't coming into this,' Hamish said wearily. 'For heaven's sake—what was between us lasted three short weeks and was over five years ago. Over, Lilly. You needn't think I'll throw it up at you— or try and rekindle dead fires. I'm not that stupid—and I'm sure not in the market for any more relationships. But I don't have a choice, Lilly. I have to insist that you stay.'

This time there was no disguising the absolute exhaustion in Hamish's voice. 'There's no choice,' he repeated.

The weariness had to be ignored. 'What was between us was over five years ago. . .' Maybe. For Hamish those weeks five years ago were obviously one short interlude—one more relationship out of many—but for Lilly. . .

Lilly drew herself up to her full five feet six inches and tried for a glare. 'Hamish, you can't make me.'

'No.' Hamish dug his hands deep in his pockets. He glanced across at the burly ferry-master who was listening with undisguised curiosity. 'I can't make you. You can get back on the ferry and fight me in the courts and maybe you'll win. But I can ask you, Lilly.'

'Then I refuse. You'll find someone else,' Lilly told him in a small, hard voice. 'Dr McVie said that if he advertised he'd be swamped by applicants.'

'That might be,' Hamish said heavily. 'But it'll take a couple of weeks and I don't have that time. Angus had another coronary two days ago. It was minor but he's bedridden and I'm working alone—and I have an epidemic on my hands.'

'An epidemic?' Hamish suddenly had the full attention of both Lilly and the ferry-master. 'Of what?' Lilly asked, her tone frankly laced with disbelief.

'Diphtheria.'

Lilly stared.

'Diphtheria. . .' The ferry-master gave a long, low whistle. 'You're kidding, Doc.'

'No.' Hamish was still watching Lilly as he turned to the boatman. 'The lab in Cairns rang half an hour ago with the results of the samples you took over for me. When I suspected the first case I took swabs from everyone. There're five people who are swabbing positive and who are now showing signs of the disease and another I'm sure is the carrier.'

Silence.

The ferry-master finally broke it. He cleared his throat, obviously trying to come to grips with what he'd heard.

'But. . . Do you really reckon it's an epidemic, then, Doc? When I took the swabs over to the mainland for you, you said there was just one kiddie you were worried about.'

'Well, now there are four,' Hamish said heavily. 'And one adult.'

'All from the resort?'

'Yes.'

'Strewth.' The boatman whistled. 'But you'll ship them over to Cairns hospital quick smart, though, won't you, Doc?' the ferry-master demanded. 'Diphtheria. . . Heck, my mum tells stories of diphtheria. It killed two kiddies in her family—but I thought it was a thing of the past.'

'It nearly is,' Hamish agreed. Hamish was still watching Lilly as he spoke, his face grim and drawn. Lilly was a complication he hadn't needed, his face told her.

'So why the epidemic?' Lilly demanded. The doctor in Lilly was surfacing whether she willed it or not as she asked the question.

'There's a religious group staying at the resort who believe in minimal medical intervention,' Hamish told her. 'None of their children have been immunised, and most of the adults' childhood immunisation has lapsed. They don't believe in hospitals and they say they're staying right here—and they'll take care of their children themselves.'

'By themselves?' Lilly frowned in disbelief.

'Oh, they'll allow me to administer antitoxin and penicillin. The word diphtheria has a certain ring to it that's made even the most anti-medical of them think twice,' Hamish said grimly. 'But they're not afraid enough—yet—to consider hospitals, no matter what I say. So. . . They're staying in self-contained cabins on the north of the island. We've run a quarantine barrier on the road in—and we'll go from there.' Hamish faced to confront Lilly full on.

'But, like it or not, I need you, Dr Inger. Desperately. Angus has done us no favours, but I believe we have to like it or lump it. So let's get your bags up to the house.'

I need you. . . Desperately. . .

He did. Lilly looked up at Hamish's exhausted eyes—at the hand that ran through his flaming hair— and her anger and despair receded a little. Just a little. Enough, though, to put things in perspective.

Angus McVie had set them up. She was sure of it. Given her druthers, Lilly would hightail it out of here just as fast as her legs would carry her. She'd swim if she had to.

But there was Davey to consider, and there was this man's need.

Diphtheria. . . Lilly had never treated a case. She'd never even seen a case. With inoculation it was considered nearly eradicated.

With the fear of the disease diminishing, so too was

caution. As memories of the dreadful diphtheria epidemics faded to crumbling gravestones, the need to inoculate became less and less obvious.

Lilly had read in her medical journals that the incidence of the disease was on the rise again for this very reason.

Diphtheria was a frightening disease. Its worst forms often ended in death by slow suffocation due to membranes growing over the throat, or death by myocarditis. . .

Lilly's inoculations were up to date. She did a fast review of Davey's status. No danger there. . .

So there was no reason why she should refuse to stay. No reason except that it would mean working side by side with this man. With Hamish Campbell. With a man who had betrayed her in the worst possible way.

There were four children ill. And one adult. A closed community of unvaccinated children meant that more would follow.

Hamish was right. If she had to live with her conscience she had no choice. No choice at all. . .

Hamish Campbell had taught her to care, and his teaching was now so much a part of her that she couldn't betray it.

Lilly closed her eyes. 'Of course,' she said bleakly. 'I guess I'll stay as long as you need me. But. . .but only for the diphtheria outbreak.'

'Generous of you,' Hamish said drily, and Lilly winced at the scorn in his voice. Hamish was already turning to the ferry-master, though. 'Charlie, could you take Dr Inger up to the house. I have to get back to. . .'

And then he stopped in mid-sentence.

'I can't find your coat and I've searched and searched,' Davey announced from the cabin door. 'Mummy, are you sure you left it there?'

Hamish's face froze as he turned toward the child's voice. The young doctor looked down at the little boy as if he was seeing a ghost—and Davey looked uncertainly back at him.

'Well, will you look at that?' the ferry-master exclaimed. 'If it don't beat all. . .' His eyes moved from Davey to Hamish and back to Davey. 'I noticed the kid's hair and eyebrows when he got on board the boat, but it didn't click till now. Matching flame-red and black! When the kid grows up he's going to be an almost dead ringer for Doc Campbell!'

Silence.

This wasn't real, Lilly thought desperately. It was a nightmare. . .

This was a nightmare Lilly had relived over and over for nearly five long years. One day she'd known it must happen—but even with five years' preparation she still felt like she'd been knocked sideways.

She watched the exhaustion on Hamish Campbell's face turn to incredulity as he stared down at Davey—and then slowly Hamish turned to her.

He opened his mouth to speak but Lilly was before him.

'We're wasting time,' she said savagely—desperately. 'If you've an epidemic to cope with then you must be needed elsewhere, Dr Campbell. I'm sure Charlie will give me all the help I need in finding the place where you've arranged for me to stay.'

Hamish ignored her. He crossed to the child and smiled down at Davey, their matching heads of flame striking in the brilliant sunshine. 'Hi,' Hamish said softly. He stooped and held out his hand in a gesture of man-to-man welcome. 'I'm your mum's new partner, Dr Hamish Campbell. Welcome to Nooluk.'

'Hi,' Davey said gamely and proffered his fingers.

'Who do I have the honour of addressing?' Hamish asked solemnly. 'I've told you my name. . .'

Davey looked wonderingly up at him but Hamish's smile gave nothing but reassurance.

It did that to people, Lilly thought bitterly. Hamish's

smile. . . He could talk anyone into anything with that smile.

Davey was no exception. He placed his small hand into Hamish's larger one with care and solemnly shook it.

'You're my mum's new partner?'

'Yep.'

Davey nodded. 'Then I guess it's OK to tell you my name,' he decided gravely. 'I'm David Campbell Inger and I'm four.'

David Campbell Inger. Aged four. Button-nosed, freckled—and a tiny, younger version of the man kneeling beside him.

The ferry-master's jaw dropped about a foot. With man and child side by side, there were some questions that didn't need to be asked.

There were some facts that couldn't be denied.

'Lilly. . .' Hamish's voice held a note of stunned wonder. He looked down at Davey and it was like a man beholding a miracle.

'No!' Lilly said the word desperately, cutting off Hamish's exclamation almost before it was out. She crossed fast to lift Davey, snatching him away from Hamish's clasp and hugging him close as a barrier between herself and those questioning eyes. The questions would have to be answered, she knew—but not yet.

'Please. . .please go back to your work,' she said miserably—as loud as she could make her voice work through a throat that felt dry and sore and tighter than she'd ever known it to feel. 'Please. . . We don't need you, Dr Campbell.'

We don't need you.

The ferry-master stirred from his trance. He looked from man and child across to Lilly and his lips parted, but whatever he'd been going to say was cut off.

The still of the morning was suddenly broken by the shattering roar of a helicopter passing low overhead.

The machine was coming in low, to land just by the jetty.

'What the heck. . .?' The ferry-master stared. 'That's the air ambulance,' he said as the noise finally abated. 'I thought you said. . .'

Hamish turned from Davey with an almost tangible effort. 'They're bringing the antitoxin,' he said. 'And more medical supplies I ordered. I. . .I'll have to go. . .'

Thank heaven for that, Lilly breathed.

The only problem was that Hamish Campbell didn't have to go far enough!

CHAPTER TWO

THE doctors' home was beautiful.

It was beautiful in every sense of the word. The building was two-storeyed, long and gracious, with a veranda running the full length of the ground floor and a wide balcony running around the upper level. Surrounding it was over an acre of lush, tropical garden running down to the beach.

Angus had said that the house could hold a score of people and Lilly could well believe it. The gracious old building had been built in the days of entertaining on a grand scale, and it still held an air of generous welcome.

If Hamish hadn't met her on the boat, Lilly would have smiled in delight at such a house. As it was, Lilly helped the ferry-master unload her belongings into the hall and listened to the housekeeper welcome her while her heart thudded with blind pain. There was room for nothing else.

'My dear, we're ever so pleased to have you here,' the housekeeper exclaimed as the ferry-master finally made his way home to his dinner and left Lilly to Mrs Price's ministrations. 'Dr McVie's been so anxious. Our Dr Angus has been asking every five minutes whether you're here yet. It was almost as though he thought you'd bolt before you got here.'

I wonder why that was? Lilly thought bleakly as she followed the housekeeper upstairs.

Like the house, their rooms were lovely.

'A balcony,' Davey whooped. 'Our very own balcony. And we can see the sea. And there's bannisters on the stairs too, Mummy—just look. Can I slide down? Please? Please?'

'There's a very large knob at the bottom of the

bannisters, young Davey,' Mrs Price said firmly. She crossed her arms over her bosom and tried to look stern. It didn't quite come off. This middle-aged lady was born for twinkling.

'If you come downstairs with me I'll explain the consequences of hitting large wooden knobs with speed right where it hurts most,' she smiled. 'And then you can have a piece of my home-made chocolate cake and a glass of milk. Would you like that?'

'Yes, please,' Davey said with enthusiasm and Lilly realised that in Mrs Price Davey was soon to have a friend.

If their stay was long enough.

'There's a pot of tea waiting for you too, Dr Inger,' Mrs Price said diffidently, 'but Dr Angus is in bed at the end of the hall and I know he's aching to see you.'

I'll just bet he is, Lilly acknowledged and sighed. Mrs Price was looking at her anxiously, though, so she summoned a smile.

'Of course, I'll go,' she assured her. 'And, please— call me Lilly.'

'It'll be my pleasure,' Mrs Price said roundly. 'And may I say what a pleasure it is to have you and the wee one here. When Dr Angus told me we had a young lady with a wee boy taking the job you could have knocked me over with a feather I was that pleased. Since Dr Angus had his heart attack this place's been like a morgue.'

'Dr McVie's heart problem shouldn't have made Dr Campbell all that quiet, should it?' Lilly asked before she could help herself, and the housekeeper shrugged.

'Our Dr Hamish's always been a quiet one,' Mrs Price sighed. 'He has ghosts, that one. His lovely wife died, you know. That was three years before he came here but he still feels it, poor man.' She straightened and seemed to brace her shoulders. 'Well, come on, then, young Davey, and catch this chocolate cake before it gets stale. That's a fate no chocolate cake deserves!'

They trooped off down the staircase and Lilly listened to their retreating laughter with misgivings.

This place seemed so right.

It wasn't right. This place was all wrong. Of all the places in Australia Lilly least wanted to be, this island had to take the prize.

It was no use thinking like that now. She was stuck. For the duration of the diphtheria epidemic, Lilly Inger just had to make the best of a bad job. A very bad job. . .

Angus McVie was waiting. His bedroom was at the end of the hall, Mrs Price had told her. OK.

If she was to make the best of this, Lilly first had to face the man who'd put her in this position. Boy, did he have some explaining to do!

Lilly took three deep breaths, tried for a spot of mental bracing and stalked down the corridor as angry as she had ever been in her life. She stopped at the front bedroom, tapped lightly and went inside and her anger faded as soon as she saw the man in the bed.

It was six weeks since Lilly had seen the elderly doctor and in that time Angus McVie seemed to have shrunk. He lay back on a mound of white pillows, his white hair almost disappearing against the linen, and his eyes, as Lilly opened the door, were so absurdly anxious that Lilly found herself tempted to smile.

He looked like a small, elderly, pyjama-clad gnome—a garden gnome facing a bulldozer.

'Dr McVie. . .' Lilly meant her voice to sound cross, but it didn't come out that way. This man was too ill for anger.

'Lilly.' Angus McVie's anxious old eyes perused hers and he held out hands that shook with weakness. 'Welcome, girl.'

Lilly bit her lip. She crossed to the bed, took his hands and sat down on the covers. 'I'm not very welcome,' she said bluntly. 'Angus McVie, you are a devious, interfering, lying. . .'

'I didn't lie,' he said indignantly and then he looked

up at her drawn face. 'I'm sorry, lass,' he told her, 'but it seemed. . .it seemed. . .'

'Like a good idea?' Lilly asked incredulously. 'To throw together two people who you must know parted in anger—and parted nearly five years ago with no contact since? Dr McVie, Hamish and I had a relationship which ended dreadfully. If I'd known he was here. . .' She sighed. 'You must know he feels the same,' she said softly. 'So why did you do it?'

'He still loves you.'

'Well, that's a nonsense.'

'It's no nonsense, girl,' Angus told her steadily. 'I know my nephew.'

'No.'

Lilly rose a trifle unsteadily and walked over to the window. The view over the beach and out to sea was truly breathtaking but Lilly hardly saw it. 'Dr McVie, Hamish—your nephew—and I had an affair which lasted three weeks,' she said at last. 'Three weeks, for heaven's sake! And now, five years later, you tell me he still loves me. You expect us to pick up the pieces of a long past affair. Or. . .or pretend nothing happened.'

'If it meant so little to you, then you will be able to pretend nothing happened,' the old man said roundly. 'If I'm wrong about the way my nephew feels. . .'

'Look, I don't know what Hamish has told you about me. . .'

Angus shook his head. His old eyes were distressed. 'Lilly, Hamish is my sister's son,' he said softly. 'His mother told me there was a girl—a student doctor—he met when the girl was assigned to follow his work for a few weeks five years ago. His mother said Hamish was another person after he met her. She saw him a couple of times when the girl was with him and he seemed—well, for a while she thought he was human again.

'Only then Lauris came back and it ended. His mother didn't know any details. We assumed. . . We assumed

the problems with Lauris were too great. But now that
Lauris is dead. . .'

'You thought you'd come and find me and throw me
in Hamish's direction again.'

'Well. . .'

'Dr McVie, have you any idea how complicated this
all is?' Lilly asked. 'How on earth did you find me?'

'Easy.' Angus spread his hands. 'I knew it was fifth-
year students who are assigned to follow the work of
practising doctors and Hamish's mother knew the
approximate dates. I knew which university used the
region Hamish was working in and I know the professor
of general practice at your university.' He gave a tired
smile. 'Also, I borrowed a photograph.'

'A photograph?'

'Hamish keeps it in his desk drawer,' Angus said
simply. 'All the time.'

'I. . .I see,' Lilly said slowly. She shook her head,
trying to clear her thoughts. The fact that Hamish had
kept her photograph didn't matter one bit. It couldn't
be allowed to matter. 'So. . .'

'So I wrote to your professor and I found he knows
you well and is fond of you. He told me you were
thinking of a country career—so the rest seemed easy.'

'I. . .I see.' Lilly turned back to face him. 'I see.
But. . .but what about Davey?'

'I hadn't counted on Davey,' the old man admitted.
His eyes rested on Lilly's face. 'You have no idea how
much he threw me when I met the lad. Is he really
Hamish's son?'

'What do you think?' Lilly said wearily. 'Dr McVie,
I wish you hadn't done this.'

Angus looked up into Lilly's pale face and his lips
tightened. 'I don't,' he said at last. 'Hamish didn't know
about the little boy—about his son—did he?'

'No. At least. . .not until half an hour ago. I doubt I
can keep it from him now.'

'You don't think he has the right to be a father to the child?'

'Hamish Campbell has no rights,' Lilly said bleakly. 'He seduced me when he was in a position of power and I was a kid. A student! You have no idea, Dr McVie. Your nephew. . . Well, I though he was such a fine doctor. He was so gentle. . .so caring. . .' Lilly cut the words off with a sharp tightening of her lips. Remembering was the way of agony. 'My aunt—my only relative—had just died,' she explained slowly. 'I was alone and unhappy and I thought he loved me. I would have given him the world. And then. . .' she gave a hard, self-mocking laugh '. . .and then I found he was married. "Married surgeon has casual fling with student!" Age-old story. And there's never a happy ending.'

'Why didn't you tell him about the bairn?' Angus asked slowly and Lilly shook her head.

'He had no right to know. He betrayed me.'

'But you still carried his child. You could have had an abortion—or had it adopted.'

'No.'

'No choice?'

'No choice,' Lilly said bleakly.

'Because you still love the bairn's father?'

'No!' Lilly shook her head again. 'That's nonsense. I was a silly kid once, but no more.'

'How old were you, Lilly? How old were you when you fell in love with my nephew?'

'Twenty-two.' She shook her head. 'Old enough to know better. Maybe old enough for Hamish to expect I could take care of myself. But still. . .still a stupid kid, for all that.'

'I see.' The tired old eyes perused Lilly's face with care. 'So, what will you do now, girl? Sue the pants off me?'

Lilly managed a smile, her natural humour surfacing for a fleeting instant. 'I like you better with your pants on,' she admitted. 'Even if they are pink striped pyjamas.' Her smile faded. 'I gather there's a medical emergency on the island now. I'm more or less being blackmailed into staying until it's over—but then Davey and I will go back to the mainland.'

'The professor told me the practice you were in gave you the option to stay.'

'It doesn't matter,' Lilly said bleakly.

'It does matter,' Angus told her. He reached out a gnarled hand once more and, after a moment's hesitation, Lilly moved to take it in hers. He gripped her with surprising strength.

'Lass, I know I didn't tell you the whole truth,' he said softly, 'but I meant it for the best. Hamish—well, he's a good lad. He came here when I most needed him and as for that wife of his—well, he's been through hell and back. I doubt if you know the half of it. But I never meant to hurt you, girl, and that's the truth.

'Lilly, stay for two weeks at least—until this damned epidemic is under control—and have out what you need to have out with my nephew. At the end of two weeks, I'll pay your expenses in finding another position on the mainland. I promise. But I'm asking you, Lilly. Pleading, if you like. Give us two weeks. Please. . .'

Lilly looked down into the old man's eyes, trying for anger and succeeding only in feeling compassion.

OK, this man had caused her no end of heartache but he hadn't done it for his own devious ends. He loved his nephew. And by the look of him he might not even be alive in two weeks.

Two long weeks. . .

Well, now that Hamish knew about his child she'd have to face him and maybe—maybe Angus was right. Maybe she should have given Hamish the opportunity to know his son. It wasn't just Lilly whose rights were being questioned here. Davey had rights, too, and one of those rights was to know his father.

Two weeks should do that, she thought grimly. Two long weeks.

Angus McVie was holding her hand still, his old eyes pleading, and Lilly finally found herself smiling reassurance.

'Two weeks, then,' she said softly. 'But only two. And that's the end of it, Angus McVie. I swear. . .'

Lilly was determined to unpack only the bare essentials so unpacking took her less than half an hour. Then she changed into a more serviceable skirt and blouse, twisted her hair into a knot and felt better. She was here to work and her sensible clothes helped her feel a bit more in control of this crazy situation.

She was here to work. Nothing else.

Finally she went downstairs—to find Davey making chocolate chip cookies with Mrs Price.

'Mrs Price let me tip the whole packet of chocolate bits in,' Davey crowed as Lilly entered the kitchen. 'Mrs Price says why don't we just call them chocolate blobs and forget about calling them cookies? And I'm allowed to lick the bowl.'

The housekeeper glanced at Lilly's strained face and moved over to lift a large teapot from the hob.

'Now, you just hush your chattering and put nice round teaspoons of mixture on the tray, Master Davey,' she said soundly. 'Tea, lass? And lots of sugar, by the look of you.'

Lilly sipped her tea gratefully, sitting back and listening to her son's idle chatter while her heart tried to come to grips with what had happened.

It was too much. She felt like the breath had been knocked out of her, and she didn't have a clue how to recover her equilibrium.

Finally she rose, washed her mug and walked over to stare out of the window.

The garden really was beautiful.

It was hard to concentrate on a garden, no matter how beautiful it was.

Finally the phone cut across her wayward thoughts. Lilly turned to find Mrs Price holding out the receiver for her.

'It's Dr Hamish,' she smiled.

Hamish.

Lilly took the receiver like she'd receive a chalice of poison, and cautiously raised it to her ear.

'Yes?'

'Dr Inger, are your inoculations up to date?'

There was no pleasant greeting here. This was cold. Formal. Work. There was enough strain in Hamish's snapped words to make Lilly focus absolutely.

'I had combined diptheria-tetanus last time I needed a tetanus booster,' Lilly told him. ADT protected against diphtheria as well as tetanus. Once regarded as standard, it was more and more regarded as unnecessary. 'That was only last year so, yes.'

'Then I need you. Now.'

'What's wrong?'

'Everything,' Hamish told her harshly. He was speaking over background noise—a child sobbing and a woman's voice trying to comfort. 'Lilly, things are getting out of control here. I've a four-year-old whose breathing's threatening to fail and a woman whose heart's being affected by this damned disease. Her husband won't agree to her having an electrocardiograph so I don't know how bad she is, but I'm suspecting the worst.'

'She's too ill to consent herself?' Lilly asked, frowning.

'You don't know this group,' Hamish said grimly. 'What the men say goes—and the leader's the worst of the lot of them. The lady with the heart condition is the leader's wife and she just lies there and stares at the ceiling. Her husband answers every question for her until I'm ready to throttle him. I also have three other kids growing worse while I watch and even though their mothers are scared out of their wits they won't stand up to the men.'

Hamish paused and Lilly could imagine him running his hand through his hair in a gesture of weariness and frustration. 'Lilly, I need you,' he repeated.

'Of course I'll come, Hamish.'

Lilly bit her lip. She'd meant to be formal. She'd meant to call this man Dr Campbell and nothing else. The 'Hamish' had slipped out of its own volition.

Hamish Campbell hardly heard. He was totally caught up in his medical need and what Lilly called him was pure irrelevance.

'I hoped to give you an hour or so to settle,' he continued, 'but the only nurse with up-to-date vaccinations was here with me all night. She came back while I organised supplies and met you from the boat but now she's collapsed, exhausted. I had to send her home, which means I'm on my own, and this situation is looking more grim by the minute. Can you come now?'

'Yes.' She couldn't think of this man as Davey's father now. This was a medical nightmare and everything else was shoved aside.

Later their own personal tension could surface again, but both doctors were trained to focus on imperatives. 'Hamish, do you need me to bring anaesthetic equipment? Are you preparing the child for a tracheotomy?'

'I have what I need here,' Hamish told her, his voice tight with strain. 'Not that I can use it. The group's leader refuses to let me anything at all! His wife is the only ill adult, but he doesn't seem the least worried.'

'And he won't let you insert a tracheostomy tube if you need to?'

'No.' The word was practically a groan. 'Even though the child's throat is becoming more blocked by the minute. If I wait much longer it'll be an emergency procedure when the child's breathing fails completely—and I'll bet they let me operate when that happens,' Hamish added bitterly. 'But I need you here, Lilly. To operate on my own. . . And if the woman's heart fails. . .'

Hamish broke off, sheer exhaustion making his voice falter over the last few words.

His nurse had collapsed exhausted because she'd been up all night.

Hamish must have been up all night too. And maybe the night before that.

'I'm coming. Just tell me where to go.'

'You'll have to drive Angus's car. . .'

'No worries.'

'That's what you think,' Hamish retorted and, amazingly, there was a faint trace of laughter in his voice. It faded almost as soon as Lilly imagined it. 'Just drive north to resort and they'll direct you from there. But come as fast as you can.'

Hamish needed her.

Of course she'd come.

CHAPTER THREE

FROM the other side of the kitchen Mrs Price was watching Lilly, her face creased in concern as the conversation continued.

Davey's teaspoons of cookie mixture were growing to tennis-ball size and she hardly noticed.

'Trouble?' she asked as Lilly replaced the receiver.

'You might say that,' Lilly said grimly, still staring down at the phone. 'I have to go.'

The woman sighed. 'I gathered. I do hope you can make Dr Hamish come home for some sleep. The man's not slept for days and I've hardly seen him except when he rushes back for surgery. He's due back for evening surgery at seven, but if the diphtheria is spreading. . . Maybe I should ring round and cancel.'

'Leave it for the time being,' Lilly told her. 'Maybe I can get back to do it. Mrs Price, Hamish said I should drive Dr McVie's car.'

'Dr Angus's car. . .' Mrs Price's eyes widened. 'I guess. . .I suppose that's all there is, but are you sure you're brave enough to drive such an extraordinary vehicle?'

It was indeed an amazing car.

Dr Angus McVie drove a magnificent, gleaming Model T Ford, manufactured in 1924 and kept in mint condition since.

'It was Dr Angus's father's before him,' Mrs Price told Lilly, leading her out to the garage. 'He had it since new.'

'Good grief!' Lilly stared in stupefaction. 'Is it. . .? I mean, does it go?'

'It surely does,' Mrs Price said roundly. 'And I

popped upstairs to check and Dr Angus said of course you're to drive it and he said he has great faith in your ability to do anything you set you mind to. It's easy to drive—according to our Dr Angus, though I wouldn't get behind the wheel if you paid me—and he said the car will enjoy the experience even if you don't.'

It seemed that there was no choice. Lilly took a deep breath. She stared uncertainly at her amazing method of transport, her mouth twitched at the corners in the beginning of laughter—and she gave it a whirl.

If she hadn't been trying to drive fast, it would have been an absolute delight.

Behind the wheel, Lilly might have been back in the nineteen-twenties. She puttered north across the island in her wonderful car and if so much hadn't been happening in her crowded mind she would have laughed out loud in delight.

This island was straight out of a fairy tale—with vast patches of nightmare thrown in.

The resort was about a mile from the doctors' home. TURTLE BAY the sign on the imposing entrance announced. The resort looked lush, magnificent and very, very expensive.

Lilly parked her wonderful car beside an artificial waterfall and made her way to Reception.

'I need to know where Dr Hamish Campbell is,' she said to the girl at the desk, and immediately a smart-suited young man broke away from a group of guests and made a beeline for Lilly. She was taken by the arm and ushered with little ceremony into a side room.

'Who are you?' the man asked abruptly, with no attempt at civility.

'I'm Dr Inger.' Lilly looked down at the oily little man and frowned. She wasn't used to this sort of reception. 'If you could just tell me. . .'

'Another blasted doctor. . . I thought I told you people to use the staff entrance,' the man snarled. 'If word gets round as to what those people have. . . We'll be ruined, that's what we'll be. One hint of dip...of *that* disease and people will leave by the droves.'

'The patients aren't in the main building, then?' Lilly asked.

'They wouldn't be anywhere near the place if I could help it,' Oil-Head snapped. 'But they paid for their full stay in advance and Dr Campbell says I can't evict them. And, no, they're not in the main building, thank heaven. We have a series of self-contained cabins down on Turtle Point. They booked the lot.

'Your Dr Campbell has placed barricades on the road going down there and I'm having no end of trouble answering questions as to why our guests can't walk along that road now. I've had to say it's a conservation department decree.' He ran a hand through sparse, slick hair and groaned.

'And now I suppose you'll want to go down there and then I'll get more questions as to why our house guests can't go too.'

'Yes, I do need to go down there,' Lilly said stiffly. 'Fast.'

'And how many other doctors am I expected to have traipsing through here? Look, Miss...Whatever-Your-Name-Is, these people are welcome to whatever they believe—they're welcome to die for all I care but I just want them off my patch!' He glowered.

'And before you go traipsing down there on your mission of mercy I need you for one of my regular guests, a Mr Irving—Irving Plastics, you understand—who sprained his ankle playing tennis this afternoon. Dr Campbell was called but he hasn't come.'

'Maybe Dr Campbell thought diphtheria was more urgent than a sprained ankle,' Lilly suggested drily. 'And I'm sorry, but I think so too. Now, will you give me directions—or do I walk out into the foyer and ask at the top of my lungs whether anyone knows where the hotel is keeping its diphtheria patients?' Lilly's patience had been stretched to the limit. 'You have a choice and you have two seconds to decide.'

Two minutes later, Lilly was chugging southward in her little car, directions in her hand and a sour taste in her mouth. Oil-Head stayed behind, still glowering.

The self-contained villas were easy to find. Lilly had to stop to shift and replace the sign saying PROHIBITED AREA—TURTLE HABITAT and the villas were a few hundred yards further on.

It was a wonderful place. As a retreat for a church group it was ideal, Lilly thought. Cut off from the outside world, the place had an air of tranquillity and beauty that almost took Lilly's breath away.

There were a dozen or so straw-thatched villas bordering the sand, each with a balcony overlooking the beach. Groups of adults were sitting on each balcony and a mob of sandy, happy children were tossing balls to each other in the shallows.

Paradise, Lilly thought softly, and wondered how diphtheria dared to raise its ugly head in a place like this.

She parked her crazy car with care. From the balcony she was watched by all eyes but no one came near. It was as if they were afraid.

'I'm looking for Dr Campbell,' she called to the nearest group of adults as she walked across the soft sand toward the villas. This place. . . She looked longingly down at the water and had to suppress an almost irresistible urge to kick her shoes off, head to the water and dip her toes in the rushing surf.

Cut it out, Lilly, she told herself severely. Doctors didn't paddle—at least doctors with diphtheria epidemics in front of them didn't paddle!

Finally a man came forward in time to save Lilly from her crazy impulses and gestured her to the end of the row of villas.

'Doc Campbell's down there.'

Seen at close quarters, it was obvious that all was

not well in paradise. The man's face was grim and
drawn and Lilly was right about her first impression of
fear. It was almost tangible.

'No one's to go down there,' the man told her. 'The
doctor has it quarantined.'

'My inoculations are up to date,' Lilly reassured him.
'I'm another doctor.'

The man's expression cleared a shade—from terrified to just plain frightened. 'Well, you're welcome,
Doctor, and that's a fact,' he said simply. 'I'm Greg
Denton. My son's one of the sick children. I've two
others to care for or I'd be with him, but my wife's
down there trying. . .trying to help.' He grimaced. 'I'd
be grateful if you could tell me how you find him.
Tommy. He's. . .he's four. . .'

Lilly's heart sank. Tommy must be the child Hamish
had told her about.

'Tommy's the child who needs the tracheotomy tube
to help him breathe?' Lilly said tentatively and watched
the frightened face close.

'Mr Gibbs says he doesn't need it.'

'Who's Mr Gibbs? Is he a doctor?' Lilly asked
politely.

'No. But he says. . . He says everything will be OK.
Mr Gibbs reckons Tommy's a good kid and he's too
young to be punished.'

Lilly swallowed. So this was what Hamish was
facing. She glanced across at the villa the man had
directed her to and then took a deep breath. Maybe she
could do more good out here for the moment. It was
worth a try.

'You mean you and your wife haven't given permission for the tracheotomy?' she asked.

'Louise. . . My wife wants to but Mr Gibbs said not.'

There was just enough uncertainty—just enough
naked fear—in the man's voice to make Lilly continue.

'So, because Mr Gibbs told you not to be frightened,
everything's OK?' she asked softly.

'N-no.' The man's voice broke and he turned away. 'Yes. Please. . . Doctor, I don't know what to think.'

'Mr Denton, I've been speaking to Dr Campbell by phone and he tells me Tommy's getting worse,' Lilly told him bluntly. 'There's a thick membrane growing over Tommy's throat and his breathing's almost completely blocked. If it blocks completely then he'll die. We need to insert a tube—make a small slit in his throat and bypass the membrane so he can breathe—but we can't do it without your permission.'

'I can't give it,' the man said heavily, his back to her.

'Mr Denton, I don't want to question your beliefs.' Lilly's voice softened still further, aware that other adults were approaching and straining to hear.

'But to say Tommy's safe because he's a good kid. . . Mr Denton, thousands—thousands—of tiny children too young to be anything but good kids have died in the past of diphtheria. Modern medicine offers some hope, but to refuse medicine. . . The reason thousands of children no longer die is almost purely down to the treatment you're refusing.'

'But. . .I don't want to refuse. . .' The man put a hand to his head in a gesture of absolute bewilderment. 'I just don't know. . .'

Around him, a cluster of adults and a few straggling children were now watching with sympathetic eyes.

'Why don't you give Tommy the best chance you can?' Lilly said gently. 'Surely you can do that? Surely it doesn't go so strongly against what you believe to let him go to hospital? To let Tommy be cared for by men and women skilled in the management of this awful disease?'

'But. . .' the man's voice broke on a sob. 'You don't understand. . .'

'I understand.'

The new voice came from a pale-faced, middle-aged lady speaking from the back of the group. Now the woman darted forward and put her arm round Greg

Denton's shoulders in a gesture of comfort. 'Henry Gibbs has us all in the palm of his hand, Greg, and it's time we faced it.'

'What do you mean?' Lilly asked.

'We're a small group,' the woman said softly, turning to face Lilly. 'Just a few families with the same beliefs—wanting to make this world better, if you like. Nothing radical. We all see the need to make this world safer and more. . .more moral for our kids.

'We started out as a buying co-operative working to buy bulk food so we'd avoid plastic packaging, and it went from there. Just twenty or so families in the group. It was fairly informally structured—and then came Henry Gibbs.'

'He came after you were formed?' Lilly asked.

'Ten years ago. He offered to build us a church,' the woman said bitterly. 'Oh, the money he poured into it. . . You wouldn't believe. And then my husband lost his job, and Henry found him one in the business he runs. And the Clarkes ran into financial trouble and Henry Gibbs took over the mortgage on their house. And he loaned the Dentons enough to build their house, and he's paying for all the group kids' schooling at a great little private school.

'We're getting more and more beholden—and I hadn't realised how much until now. What Henry Gibbs says goes, and the men all agree with him and if the women worry, then up till now we've shut up.'

She shook her head and her hold around Greg's shoulders tightened. 'But this hospital thing,' she continued. 'We never believed that, or at least I never did. My daughter had appendicitis the year before Henry came and we couldn't get her to hospital fast enough.

'But about eight years ago Henry Gibbs said no immunisations and he's getting more and more rigid in what he'll allow, and now even my husband's saying maybe we were wrong and Caroline's appendix would have cured itself.' She took a deep breath.

'It's as if the men are being brainwashed. And maybe. . .maybe there are more women feeling like me—that it's time to call it quits.'

Lilly nodded. 'I see. And if you disobey Mr Gibbs and take our advice, what then?'

'I guess. . .' Greg Denton finally spoke, his voice heavy and drained. He shook the woman's arm from his shoulders as though rejecting comfort. 'I guess he'll kick us out of the group. Foreclose on the mortgage. We'll lose our house and my kids won't be able to go the school we all send them to.'

'And if there's a choice?' Lilly said gently. 'A choice between losing your house and losing your son. . .?'

Greg Denton's eyes flew up to hers. 'It's not as bad as that.' He sounded as if he didn't really believe what he was saying but he had to say it anyway. 'It's not. It's only the women, panicking. . .'

'It is as bad as that,' Lilly told him. 'I'm sorry, but I think you must face it—before Tommy dies and you're forced to face it then. If the women are panicking then they're right to do so. Your children aren't immunised and they're susceptible to a disease that kills. Do you believe Mr Gibbs enough to watch your children die?'

The ensuing silence seemed to last forever. There was more than one sick child and Lilly could guess, looking round at the ashen faces, which were the parents facing immediate life and death decisions.

'You say. . . You're sure Tommy has to have a tracheotomy now?' Greg Denton finally said.

'I haven't seen Tommy—but Dr Campbell seems sure.'

'And you'll agree with Dr Campbell?'

'Dr Campbell is a skilled and experienced surgeon,' Lilly said softly. 'If he thinks Tommy needs it, then I'd imagine he'll be right. Tommy needs a tracheotomy— but he'd be much safer if he had it in a mainland hospital.'

'But you can do it here?'

Lilly hesitated. 'I guess. . . If we must.'

'Then do it here,' the man said heavily. 'Tell Louise. . . Tell my wife I said she's to give her permission. She wanted me to but. . .I don't know. . . Gibbs said. . . Gibbs said the men have to make the decisions. Look, somehow I'll square it with Gibbs afterwards. But no hospital. Not yet. . .'

It was a minor victory but at least she'd gained some concession. Lilly walked across to the end villa with a lighter heart, knowing that she was the bearer of at least a little good news.

Hamish certainly needed it.

The weary doctor looked up from what he was doing as Lilly entered, and his strongly boned face seemed to sag in relief at the sight of her.

'Lilly. . .'

The softly spoken word cut through Lilly's heart like a knife, for one horrible moment slashing through the medical drama and cutting her to the bone.

Hamish Campbell had spoken her name like that every time he'd seen her all those years ago. He'd whispered it every time she'd woken by his side. . .

She had to shake herself to make herself believe that this was five years on—and the way he said her name was now only expressing relief.

It had never meant more than relief or casual affection. The time for being a fool was over!

Lilly shoved her mind back to the present with an angry jerk. Now was hardly the time for this emotional garbage.

Hamish had changed since Lilly had seen him on the ferry. His casual trousers and shirt were now covered in a medical white coat, but it wasn't just the clothes that had changed. Every trace of the relaxed man Lilly had seen on Nooluk wharf had disappeared.

He must have relaxed only for a moment then, she realised, recognising a trick she'd learned in long stints in Casualty. Five minutes of blocking out drama and making her body relax absolutely could be made to equal almost an hour's sleep.

Hamish Campbell had relaxed for five minutes while he waited for the ferry—but his five minutes had to make up for days with no sleep.

He certainly wasn't relaxed now. His focus was all on work and his face, after his initial relief at seeing another doctor, was tightening again to a look as grim as Lilly had ever seen.

Hamish bent back over the nearest bed, allowing Lilly to enter without saying another word. Lilly gazed round slowly, her heart sinking.

If paradise was outside, the awfulness of this place more than made up for it.

The villa had a long living-room-cum-kitchen with two bedrooms and a bathroom leading off at the back. Lilly couldn't see what was in the bedrooms but the sight meeting her eyes in the living-room was bad enough.

There were five beds stretched in a row as a makeshift hospital ward. Each bed held a patient in various stages of disease.

There was a child on the nearest bed. A little boy. It didn't take brains to realise that this was Tommy. The child was deathly pale, semi-conscious and fighting desperately for each breath. Hamish had obviously been working on him when Lilly entered. Now he returned to his work, bending over the child and adjusting the pillows so that the child's chest wasn't bent.

There was a woman sitting on the bed beside the child and she had to be the child's mother. Louise Denton looked nearly as exhausted as the frail Tommy, and she held the child's hand as though she was afraid to release it.

There were two other children—small girls—in the next beds who were so ill that they lay wan and listless and in the next was an older boy who was whinging to another woman.

'I only have a sore throat. I don't see why I have to stay here. Honest, Mum, I want to go back to the beach. . .' He broke off in a hoarse cough and Lilly winced.

In the last bed there was an elderly woman lying motionless under the covers and staring sightlessly up at the ceiling, her mass of white hair spread round her face like a halo. She had an oxygen mask at her side and even from here Lilly could see that her colour was awful.

The woman's face was absolutely expressionless. Odd. . . The rigidity holding her didn't seem normal. The woman's hands were clenching and unclenching on the coverlet and Lilly wondered whether she was in pain.

A gentleman of a similar age to the lady was perched on the end of her bed, serenely reading a newspaper. He seemed totally unconcerned about the woman's rigid pose. The woman didn't look in his direction at all. From here it seemed almost as if the woman was furious about something that Lilly didn't understand.

There was a lot happening here that Lilly didn't understand.

Good grief! This was a doctor's nightmare—a whole hospital ward of frighteningly ill people and no nursing assistance or any back-up. No wonder Hamish was looking grim.

He could lose every one of these patients, Lilly knew, if he wasn't permitted to treat them. And he'd faced that alone. . .

He wasn't alone now. Lilly took a deep breath, consciously stepping into professional gear, and crossed to stand by Hamish.

'How can I help?' she asked simply. She looked uncertainly across at the elderly woman. 'Would you like me to. . .'

Hamish followed her gaze and shook his head.

'Mrs Gibbs seems fine for the moment. I hope. Not

that I can tell without tests, and she'll hardly answer my questions.' His own hands clenched. 'Dr Inger, if you want to help, how are you at knocking sense into blockheads?' he asked savagely. He motioned to the man sitting on the woman's bed. 'That's Henry Gibbs. He's the group's leader or mentor or whatever and what he says goes. And he says absolutely no hospital and no tracheostomy.'

'Tommy's father has given permission for Tommy to have his tracheotomy,' Lilly said bluntly. She looked down into Louise Denton's startled eyes. 'Mrs Denton, your husband says Tommy's to have the tube inserted, no matter what Mr Gibbs says.'

The woman stared up at Lilly blindly—and then down at her small son. Her face crumpled. 'Oh, thank God. . .'

'How the hell did you manage that, Lilly Inger?' Hamish whistled. He took a deep breath. 'You're a wonder-woman. If it's true. . .'

'It's true.'

'Then what are we waiting for?' The tension was lifting from Hamish's face in a rush.

Despite her anger with this man, Lilly cringed at what he'd been facing. To watch a child die, knowing that you could help if permitted but not having that permission, would be pure, dreadful torture.

'Just one moment!'

It was an imperious command of a man accustomed to having his own way. The squat, grim-faced Henry Gibbs laid down his newspaper on his wife's bed and stalked across the room. He laid a hand on Louise Denton's shoulder in a gesture of heavy paternalism and glared. 'May I ask what you people are proposing to do?'

'Help Tommy breathe,' Hamish said bluntly. He stooped and lifted Tommy's slight body into his arms, smiling down at the child's tear-stained mother as he did. 'Louise, this is Dr Lilly Inger who'll do the anaesthetic for me. Tommy's in good hands, Louise, I promise you. Lilly's a fine doctor.' Then, as Lilly flushed to the roots of her hair, Hamish turned back to the little man. 'Mr Gibbs, if you'll excuse us. . .'

The man blocked his path completely.

'I will not excuse you. I've given no permission to operate on the boy.'

'We don't need your permission,' Hamish said bluntly. 'We have his father's. And his mother's.' He looked down at Louise Denton. 'We do have yours, don't we, Louise?'

Louise looked wildly from Henry Gibbs to her little unconscious son lying in Hamish's strong arms. She visibly braced herself.

'Yes.' There was no hesitation. 'Of course you do. I wish. . .I just wish my husband had given it earlier. But. . . But hurry. . .'

'This is nonsense,' Henry Gibbs snapped and wheeled to the door. 'I'll speak to Greg Denton myself.'

'Mr Gibbs, you're going nowhere.' Hamish's voice had gone beyond fatigue. 'Look, Mr Gibbs, when I started suspecting that Tommy had diphtheria I took swabs from every person and the only one that came back positive when they're not ill was yours. That's why you're in here, Mr Gibbs. I believe you're the carrier.

'I know you had childhood inoculation—your parents obviously had more sense than you—but it's possible to be a carrier even if you are inoculated. Now go back to your wife, sit down and shut up or I'll arrange for you to stay in isolation.'

'Your threats mean nothing to me, young man,' Henry Gibbs snapped and Hamish sighed.

'Then they should,' he said wearily. 'You might hold sway over your own little group, but I'm medical officer for the region and I'm fully in my rights to have you arrested if you take one step out of this building. So sit down and let me get on with my work.'

'You don't touch Tommy,' Gibbs spat. 'I know you doctors think you make a difference but I don't believe that for a moment.' The man shook his head very strongly as if he were speaking to a stupid child. 'There'll be no deaths. We've done nothing to deserve that.'

'But Tommy'd done nothing to deserve what's happening right now,' Louise Denton quavered. 'Mr Gibbs, he's so sick. . .'

Gibbs looked down at the frightened mother. 'Then what on earth have you and your family been doing to attract this punishment?'

'They've been getting in the way of the wrong man,' Hamish snapped furiously. Hamish's voice was that of a man pushed past endurance. 'Now let me past or I'll call in the police and have you shackled. And if I were you, I'd take good care of your wife while we're operating.'

Then, as Hamish looked down at the near-apoplectic man, his voice softened. 'Gibbs, your wife really is in danger,' he warned. 'I can't convince her to go to hospital without your permission but while Dr Inger is giving the anaesthetic and I'm operating we can't watch and you're on your own. Please. . . You won't let us see what damage is being done, but she does seem to be in pain. Use the oxygen mask if she seems distressed and call me if you need help.'

'There's absolutely no need,' Gibbs said savagely. 'Margaret's been a good and obedient wife. She's led a blameless life. We don't need you.'

He glared hard at Hamish, almost as if he hated him and then finally, finally stepped aside.

'Louise, can you. . .?' Hamish said helplessly and Louise Denton nodded.

'I'll watch Mrs Gibbs, Doctor,' Louise Denton promised, glancing over at the still rigid and silent woman on the end bed. 'But please. . .please take care of Tommy.'

Take care of Tommy. . .

Easier said than done. All they had to do was operate on one critically ill little boy.

Lilly held the door of the back bedroom as Hamish carried Tommy through, carefully closed it after him, leaned against the closed door and closed her eyes.

'Don't let Gibbs rattle you,' Hamish said gently, watching her face. His eyes narrowed. 'Lilly, are you OK?'

His voice unsettled her even further. Lilly winced and forced herself to look at him. 'Hamish, it's just. . .' She shook her head. 'This situation's hopeless. I know you told Mrs Denton I was skilled but I've only done a six-month stint at anaesthetics. Tommy's so sick! Wouldn't it be better to get an experienced paediatric anaesthetist from the mainland? Could. . .could the authorities fly someone across? And maybe a theatre sister, too?'

'And a heart specialist and a paediatrician or two and a coronary care team,' Hamish added drily. 'Lilly, they won't come and I don't blame them.' Hamish set Tommy carefully down on the bed. He must have organised the room in preparation for surgery some time previously. The bed was up on blocks to make it higher. It was too soft, but it would have to do.

'The word from the mainland authorities is that we're on our own until the group decides to take the sensible course and be evacuated,' Hamish told her. 'There are helicopters on stand-by for when they do—but I just hope to heaven we can keep them all alive until they see sense.'

'But. . .'

Hamish saw her fear. He walked across and touched her pale face lightly with his fingers—with a touch that was like a caress.

Not a caress.

A meaningless gesture of comfort. Nothing more.

'You'll do this, Lilly,' Hamish said softly, his hand

still light against her face. 'I wasn't lying to Louise when I told her you were a fine doctor. Her son's in the best hands. The best.'

Somehow Lilly managed to nod—but her face didn't regain one vestige of colour.

This man just had to touch her and she lost her professional calm—she lost any sort of calm—and her heart felt like tearing in two all over again. Just the same as it had when Hamish's wife had appeared from nowhere and torn Lilly's world apart.

She couldn't think of that now. She had to haul herself back to professionalism and put heartbreak on the back-burner.

It wasn't going to go away, though, and there were two long weeks in front of her. Two weeks of Hamish Campbell. . .

They moved fast then.

There was no choice and once Lilly accepted that fact for sure then she didn't hesitate. Emotion was put firmly aside. Lilly and Hamish moved efficiently and they moved as a team.

The first thing they did was to run through the procedure together, talking it through and concentrating totally. Once they started, each task had to be done by either Hamish or Lilly and no one else. There was no theatre sister they could depend on and if all their hands were in use when a suture was required to be tied or a piece of equipment fetched then they were in trouble.

Every procedure had to be planned down to the last detail.

As they talked, gradually Lilly's nerves disappeared. Hamish was right. She could do this.

Finally, in their makeshift theatre, Lilly gave the anaesthetic. It required absolute concentration with a child as ill as Tommy, and as the child drifted into full unconsciousness Hamish moved with a speed that showed Lilly that he knew how important it was to keep the anaesthetic to a minimum.

Tommy was so sick. . . He was so close to death to begin with. . .

And out in the ward there was a woman with a heart that was failing and no nurse to help her. There was only Louise Denton acting as a volunteer. And there were other sick children. . .

There was no space for thinking of that now. Lilly concentrated fiercely on the child's fragile air supply as Hamish carefully, skilfully, made an incision in the child's neck and inserted the tracheotomy tube into the tiny, membrane-clogged throat.

Lilly had almost forgotten Hamish Campbell's surgical skills.

Like Hamish, Lilly had once planned to be a surgeon. It seemed a long time ago now—five years ago, when the impossibility of combining specialist training and single motherhood wasn't an issue. That was why she'd asked to spend time with Hamish Campbell as a student. His reputation even then was awesome. Lilly's teachers had described Hamish Campbell as the most promising young surgeon in Australia and, watching him operate then, Lilly had silently agreed.

Nothing had changed in five years. His skills were just as remarkable now, or even more so. Whatever the reasons for Hamish Campbell's decision to leave a surgical career path and turn to general practice on this island, lack of surgical skill wasn't one of them.

Why had he left, then? Lilly wondered. This man could be commanding a huge salary if he worked as a surgeon on the mainland.

There were so many things that she didn't know about Hamish Campbell—but, then, that had always been the way of it. He kept his private life close—like being married. . .

She couldn't think of that now. Lilly's attention had to be wholly on her anaesthetic—but the edges of her mind still dwelt on the man working so skilfully beside her. It was impossible to block him out completely.

Finally the tracheotomy tube was in place and Hamish carefully taped it into secure position. Tommy's colour was improving as they watched. The child's breathing was so laboured that his body had been slowly starving for oxygen and that, in itself, would put pressure on his heart.

The taping complete, Lilly reversed the anaesthetic, keeping the child sedated enough so that he wouldn't fight the tubing. She peeled off her gloves and looked cautiously across at Hamish.

He was watching her.

'Well done.' He smiled at her with the same slow smile that had done all the damage in the first place. And Lilly was just as susceptible to that smile now as she always had been.

'W-well done youself,' she managed, a trifle unsteadily. 'Hamish. . .'

'Yes?' He was smiling still and the colour flooded into her face like the blush of a silly schoolgirl.

'One. . .one of us will have to stay here all the time now,' she said slowly, concentrating fiercely on work. 'With the tracheotomy tube in place Tommy should be in Intensive Care, being monitored every moment.'

'I know.'

Hamish's smile faded. The man was almost grey with weariness and, despite her discomfiture, Lilly felt a swift jab of pity.

'Hamish, go home and sleep,' she said softly. 'I can manage here now and if I can't then I'll call you back.'

'I'll see,' Hamish said roughly. 'Let's get Tommy back in the main room and we'll check the others.'

'I can do that,' Lilly said. By the look of Hamish he was near collapse. He should be asleep—but there was little sleep with this nightmare. . .

And then she stopped dead as the door through to the living room burst open.

It was Louise Denton.

'Dr Campbell. . .' Louise's eyes flashed past Lilly

and Hamish to her little son. 'Is Tommy... Is Tommy OK?'

'Tommy's fine, Louise,' Hamish reassured her quickly. 'What's wrong?'

It took a huge effort to go on, but somehow Louise managed it. 'Please... Please... It's Margaret Gibbs. She's so upset...'

Lilly and Hamish turned as one to stare out through the open door.

'Margaret's been getting more and more distraught,' Louise stammered. 'I could see it. And when I asked what was the matter she burst into tears. Then Henry told her not to be stupid and she tried to yell at Henry and she made herself cough so much I got scared. And now she says she won't stay here. Not with Henry. Please...'

The woman in the the end bed was indeed rising. Henry Gibbs was trying to push his wife back onto the bed and having no success at all.

'Take your hands off me,' Margaret Gibbs was gasping. 'I've had enough, Henry Gibbs. Enough! My mother always said, "Know when enough's enough," and after forty years of marriage this is it! Enough!'

Margaret Gibbs was a tiny woman, nightgowned and seemingly so frail that she'd blow over with the first wisp of a breeze, but she shoved her husband aside with even more fierceness and placed her bare feet squarely on the floor.

'Mrs Gibbs, please...' Hamish started.

Margaret Gibbs glared through the bedroom door at Hamish, anger clearly giving her strength.

'Don't "Mrs Gibbs" me, young man.' She gasped for breath, fighting for the next words. 'I was born Margaret Young and I'm thinking of reverting.' There was pain in the feeble voice, and also anger. She took two steps from the bed and then gasped as a spasm caught her across her chest.

She staggered and might well have fallen if Hamish

hadn't moved fast, catching her up and lifting her bodily back to the bed.

'I won't call you Mrs Gibbs,' Hamish told the lady gently. 'But you must stay in bed. Your heart. . .'

'My heart is beginning to hurt,' Margaret Gibbs whispered, lying like a fragile doll in his arms. 'I've been lying here trying to convince myself Henry's right and it'll get better on its own. But my throat hurts and I feel dreadful and these little ones around me are getting sicker and sicker. Henry here keeps telling me it's fine—but I'm starting not to believe him.'

Her voice weakened to a thread. 'For the first time in forty years I don't believe my husband.'

'Margaret. . .' Henry Gibbs started but Margaret Gibbs ignored him. She looked pleadingly up at Hamish. 'Do you believe him, Dr Campbell?' she asked. 'Can you be sure none of us is going to die?'

Hamish lowered the frail old lady back onto the bed. Watching him, Lilly could read his thoughts and they were moving fast. The men seemed to be the ones making decisions here—and the men were led by Henry Gibbs. If just one of the women rebelled. . . And if that woman was Henry Gibbs's wife. . .

'No, Margaret,' Hamish said softly, still holding her gaze. 'I believe you're all in grave danger, and I believe the best hope is to get you all to mainland hospital facilities.'

'Then, please. . .get us to mainland hospital facilities,' the woman gasped. 'Can you organise that, young man?'

'I can.' Hamish was pressing her gently back down on the pillows.

'Margaret, what are you saying?' Henry Gibbs gasped. 'I don't believe this.'

'Then it's time you did, Henry Gibbs,' his wife whispered. 'I've been watching Louise and you never made a move to comfort her—or even offered a prayer when these doctors operated on Tommy. And then Louise offered to sponge me down and get me a drink and she's so worried about her Tommy. . .'

The woman's voice was a thready, gasping murmur but no one in the room missed a word. The room seemed electrified. Her whisper carried to every corner and even the ill children were straining to hear.

'I guess. . .I guess I just saw red, Henry Gibbs,' she whispered flatly. 'I'm hurting and hurting and so are these children and you just blather on about fate and punishment. And I've been lying here. . .and I just decided. . .I decided that what matters isn't fate and punishment. It's caring. Louise cares and she's frightened. These doctors care and they seem frightened as well. But you aren't frightened—and you don't seem to care at all.'

She glared at her husband, grabbed the oxygen mask, took a couple of deep breaths and then faced Hamish again.

'I want you to organise me to go to hospital, young man,' she whispered. She met Hamish's eyes square on, her face resolute. 'Please. . .I'm an adult and I give my consent for whatever you think I should do. I just want. . .I just want this pain to stop.'

'Margaret, I can't promise they'll cure you on the mainland,' Hamish said gently, only a faint, lurking twinkle showing Lilly how much he appreciated this woman's bravery. To stand up to a husband like Henry. . . 'I'm not even sure what's happening with your heart to cause the pain.'

'But they have a better chance than you, young man?' she asked. Then she managed a smile. 'Meaning no offence.'

'No offence taken,' Hamish smiled back. 'And, yes, they do. You should be in a coronary care unit where you have the best possible treatment.'

'Then what are you waiting for?' Mrs Gibbs sighed, weariness overtaking her. 'Take me away,' she whispered. 'The more flashing lights and sirens the better.'

She flashed an uncertain look at her boggling husband.
'I'm a mature adult, Henry, and I don't need your permission. And if I go. . .' She smiled a little uncertainly
up at Hamish. 'If I go then surely the children's parents
will have enough sense to let them come too?'

'But I won't give my permission!' Henry Gibbs was
almost as white as his wife, his face contorted with
mingled rage and shock. 'This is nonsense. Margaret,
how dare you disobey me!'

'It's not just Margaret, Mr Gibbs. I think we're all
about to disobey you.'

Louise Denton was still in the makeshift operating
theatre with her son but the door was wide open and
she must have heard every word. Now her voice cut
across the room.

'If your wife goes to the mainland, Henry, then I
doubt my husband will let you keep Tommy here.' And
then Louise's voice firmed. 'And if Margaret's defying
her husband in this. . .' She walked to the bedroom
door, smiling a tremulous smile at Hamish and then at
Lilly. 'Tommy's a better colour already. I can see that.'

'He's breathing freely again, Louise,' Hamish
told her.

Louise took a deep breath, brushing fine blonde hair
away from tired eyes. 'I know. And I'm very, very
grateful. And I think all the women here—all of us
need to put our children first from now on. Maybe. . .
maybe it's time we had a bit of women's liberation
here, wouldn't you say, Margaret? I think it's time the
womenfolk decreed what's going to happen.'

'Louise. . .' From her bed, the old lady flashed
the young mother a look that held affection and under-
standing. She struggled for breath to say what
she must. 'Louise, I'll. . .I'll even burn my bra. . .any-
thing, if only this pain will stop. . .and the children
are safe.'

Henry Gibbs was nearly apoplectic. He turned to
Louise Denton and glared a glare that would have

melted a lesser mortal where she stood. 'If you go to hospital, young woman. . . If anyone goes near a hospital I'll withdraw every shred of financial support. . .' he spluttered. 'You just watch me. Louise Denton, you'll lose your house. . .'

'Now Henry, don't be sillier than you already have been.' Margaret whispered to her husband, her anger fading as her course of action became certain. There was the beginning of compassion through the pain in her voice.

'You know it's my money you've been playing with all these years, Henry Gibbs, even though I've always let you have your way. You think I don't remember that. I do. I've always thought it wrong to remind you of it—but I have no intention of letting you blackmail anyone into endangering people's lives with my money.'

She held out her hand to Louise in a gesture of entreaty. 'I'm just sorry, my dear, that it's taken me so long to find the courage to. . .to. . .'

'To burn your bra?' Louise crossed swiftly to the elderly lady's bed and gripped her hands. 'Hey, Margaret,' she said softly, 'you're not to get upset. Please. . . You're not the only one round here who's let her husband get a bit dictatorial. Let these doctors cure you—cure us all—and then, well, maybe we'll do a bit of discovering together. Do we really need our bras?' She gave an uncertain giggle.

'Who knows, Margaret? Let's try the sensation out together. It might be quite fun wobbling!'

The last helicopter took off two hours later.

Lilly stood beside Hamish and watched it depart. The authorities brought in the big army hospital chopper, equipped with a full medical team. A diphtheria outbreak was huge news and the government was taking it very seriously indeed.

'It'll be contained now, though,' Hamish said

wearily. 'All the outbreaks in the Western world in the last few years have been contained fast with minimal mortality. We can hope. . .'

Hope for a happy ending with no deaths. Hope that the group could come to terms with the sudden militancy of its womenfolk. Hope even that Henry Gibbs could come to terms with the wonderfully bra-less Margaret.

Lilly smiled as she saw them go, and then turned uncertainly back to Hamish.

'You go back to the house,' Hamish said in a flat, exhausted voice. 'I need to make arrangements to have this place sealed. I'll follow later.'

'No.' Lilly stood firm. She met his look and placed her hands firmly on her hips. 'It's time for this woman to try a little militancy, too. You go back to the house, Hamish Campbell. I've agreed with Dr McVie that I'll stay here for two weeks—that I'll work for you for two weeks—and that's just what I'll do. So. . .you're exhausted and I'm relatively fresh.

'There's a man at the resort with a sprained ankle I need to see, so I'll do that after I finish here, and then I'll be back in time for evening clinic. You. . .go home and go to bed. Now.'

Hamish stood looking at her, a strange expression on his face. He was looking at her as one would look at a ghost. Someone out of a long-lost past, only just remembered.

The look made Lilly hesitate. It made her step back a pace and take a deep breath, as if to ward off feelings she had no intention of allowing to take hold.

'What are you waiting for, then?' she snapped in a voice that was harder than any she could ever remember using. That look. . . The look in Hamish's eyes. . . It cut her to the bone.

Hamish shook himself like a dog shaking off water. Like a man waking from a dream and trying hard to find reality.

'I guess. . .I guess there's nothing else to do, then,' he said bleakly, and Hamish Campbell turned and left Lilly to face her work alone.

CHAPTER FOUR

LILLY returned to the house an hour later to find Mrs Price waiting.

'Dr Inger...' The middle-aged woman stood on the front step and practically wrung her hands.

'Is something wrong?' Lilly took the last few steps into the house two at a time and stopped just short of the housekeeper. 'Davey... Dr McVie...'

'It's not that, dear,' Mrs Price told her. 'They're both fine. It's just... Dr Campbell came home and went straight to bed—he said you'd offered to take evening clinic—and he looked so dreadful I didn't want to wake him, but now... Well, you should see the waiting-room. I reckon we have half the population of the island here.'

'Why, for heaven's sake?' Lilly asked, stunned.

'It's the diphtheria,' Mrs Price said savagely. 'Once the big helicopters came and started evacuating, everyone found out what was going on and all the mums are frightened and they don't know whether their kids are protected or not and they want to know the symptoms and there's a couple in hysterics because their kiddies have sore throats...'

Lilly sighed. She might have expected this. When she'd finally got back to the resort to check the injured ankle of the very important Mr Irving of Irving Plastics she'd found Mr Irving and most of the other resort guests packing and departing in haste. They'd chartered a boat and were leaving immediately, and even Lilly's dislike of the oily manager hadn't stopped her feeling a little sorry for the man.

The guests weren't listening to logical reassurance. Rats deserting a sinking ship couldn't have moved with greater speed.

'I can't see there's a need for panic,' Lilly said slowly to the housekeeper. 'Dr Campbell kept the infection well contained and it seems certain the source of the disease came from outside the island. The carrier may have held the infection for years and it was only when he was in such close contact with the non-immunised children at the camp that it became a problem. And, then, with a full blown case it's much more infectious so it'd spread quickly.'

Lilly sighed again. 'But I know. The people who have come here for reassurance will have to be checked and reassured individually. I'll shower and change and come right down.'

'I'll make you soup and a sandwich you can eat on the run,' Mrs Price told her. 'I'm just sorry I can't do more. . .'

'And. . . And Davey?'

'He's asleep already,' Mrs Price beamed. 'He's a little trooper, your son.'

Lilly gave a half-hearted smile. 'But. . . Did Hamish see him when he came back?'

'I was reading Davey a bedtime story when Dr Hamish returned,' Mrs Price told her. 'After he'd showered Dr Hamish came along to see what we were doing—and you know what he did? Tired and all, Dr Hamish took the book and finished reading it for me. Tucked the little one in and all, and it did my heart good to see.'

She cast a look at Lilly that said Mrs Price's intelligent mind was asking all sorts of questions she wasn't expecting immediate answers to, and then she nodded decisively.

'Off you go and change then, girl,' the housekeeper said firmly. 'I'll just go and shut up the panic-mongers overcrowding my nice clean waiting-room.'

By the time Lilly had finished seeing every panicking islander it was close to midnight and she was exhausted.

Not only did she have to contend with panic-mongers but there were also the blatantly curious as well.

'Our Ted saw you and your little boy get off the boat and he says your wee one is the spitting image of our Dr Campbell? You're not related are you, dear? No? Pity. Odd, though. . . I mean, our Ted says it's not every day you see colouring like that. Married are you, dear? No? Oh.'

When Lilly finally finished she was close to screaming. She emerged from the surgery to find Mrs Price waiting with hot chocolate and biscuits.

'There you go, girl,' she smiled. She looked closely at Lilly's face. 'They've been giving you a hard time, I see. It's to be expected, I suppose, but they could have given you a day's grace before putting you through the hoops. Now, off to bed with you and if anyone rings I'll tell them house calls are out of the question unless they're at death's door—and even then I want statutory declarations in triplicate to prove it. Bed. . .'

Lilly took herself wearily upstairs, wondering as she went just what Mrs Price was thinking about Davey—and his likeness to Hamish. She hadn't asked a question, but her eyes were perceptive and kindly.

Davey was in the room next to hers. Lilly bent over to check him and the child opened his eyes and smiled sleepily up at her.

'I knew you'd come. . . Hamish told me there were some really, really sick people who needed you. . .' he murmured sleepily. 'So I didn't mind.'

Hamish. . .

She couldn't get away from Hamish. Even when he wasn't there, his presence enveloped the island. Already Hamish was a strong presence in her little boy's life.

'Did. . .did Hamish read you a story?' Lilly asked as she snuggled her little son close. The thought of the children suffering from diphtheria and still fighting for their lives on the mainland made her hug her little boy even harder.

'He did.' Davey gave his Mum a perfunctory squeeze and then wriggled back down onto his pillow. 'And when you didn't come and I thought I might get upset without you, Hamish gave me a teddy. He gave me Edward.'

'A teddy. . .' Lilly stared down. On the pillow was a very scruffy brown bear, rubbed almost bald in places by lots of affection in a rather disreputable past. A bear with a history. . .

'Hamish said his name's Edward,' Davey murmured, already half-asleep. 'And Hamish said Edward was his Daddy's bear and then his Daddy gave him to him so he was Hamish's bear too when he was little just like me and he said Edward has been waiting for me for a very, very long time. And now he's found me. And Edward's really, really pleased. . .'

Davey's small arm curled round the bear in protective pleasure. Wild horses wouldn't separate boy from bear. Then the child's dark lashes fluttered downward and Davey slept.

And Lilly crept into her own bed and hardly slept at all.

Edward woke her.

The scruffy, balding bear bounced onto Lilly's bed before Davey, flung there by a small, gleeful hand.

'Wake up. Wake up. It's morning, Mummy, and the beach looks beeyootiful and Mrs Price wouldn't take me yesterday because she says there has to be someone stay in the house all the time because Dr Angus is sick but we can go now, can't we, Mummy?'

Lilly blinked and blinked again. Davey's small form landed with a thud fair in her middle and the child lifted Edward high and bounced.

'Ouch. . . Horrible child. . .'

'Please, Mummy. . . Please. . . It's really, really warm and I've got my bathers on already.'

He had. Davey's skinny body was clad only in a pair

of blue swimmers. He'd delved into their belongings
and he was holding up Lilly's bikini with glee.

'I've found yours too, Mummy,' he crowed. 'So let's
go. Let's hit the beach! Edward wants to swim.'

'I'm not exactly sure bears like swimming,' Lilly
said cautiously and Davey sighed at adult stupidity.

'Of course they don't,' he said patiently. 'But they
like watching and the best thing of all they like is sand
between their toes. So let's go!'

It was like balm to a fraught spirit.

Even if Davey hadn't pushed her into it the beach
was just what she needed, Lilly decided half an hour
later. It was still only just after seven, but the sun was
already warm with the promise of heat to come, and
the soft rays of morning light were making the gentle
waves twinkle and glisten.

Lilly lay on the warm, soft sand while Davey and
Edward buried her legs, and she gradually let her tired
mind drift into something approaching contentment.

Maybe there were some good things about being
forced to stay here. Maybe. . .

Maybe not. A low, male voice raised in greeting
made Lilly swerve her head sideways. Her legs shifted
under the mound of sand, Davey set up a howl of protest
and Lilly could only agree with him.

She didn't want her morning interrupted.

Davey wasn't protesting the intrusion, though. He
was glowering at her legs.

'You moved! Mummy, you shifted and spoiled my
burying. Now I'll have to start again.'

Lilly closed her eyes and lay back again on the sand,
willing herself to be anywhere but here.

Hamish came right on. She heard the unmistakable
sound of a large, male body sinking to sit beside her
and when she opened her eyes again Hamish
Campbell's bare torso was right in her field of vision.

Like Lilly and Davey, Hamish was also dressed—or

undressed—for swimming and it was as much as Lilly could do not to gasp aloud.

She remembered this body. She remembered this strong, tanned chest. Hamish's colouring was indeed unusual. He had the vivid red hair more commonly seen among the Irish than those with Scottish ancestry but he didn't have the Celtic fair skin or green eyes to match. His skin was so dark that the sun tanned him to gleaming bronze and his clear, perceptive eyes were almost black.

He had a good body to start with, Lilly acknowledged with a faint quiver in the recesses of her heart. He'd cared for his body, too. The clearly delineated muscles of arms and chest flowed down to narrow hips and legs build like tree trunks.

He ran for exercise, Lilly remembered. Miles. The first time she'd met him it seemed as if Hamish Campbell ran to escape all sorts of demons. Later—in the brief weeks when their relationship had settled to something approaching joy—Hamish had still run but his running changed. He'd run then like a man soaking in as much of his world as he possibly could.

She wondered how he ran now.

Hamish wasn't looking at Lilly. His eyes were all on Davey as Davey indignantly started work again.

'You've brought Edward to the beach, I see,' Hamish said gravely to the child and his resonant voice still had the power to make Lilly shiver. 'That's good. Edward likes the beach.'

'I knew he would,' Davey replied, equally grave. 'Bears always do.'

'Would you like some help burying your mum?' Hamish asked. 'Do you really want to?' His eyes raked Lilly's bikini-clad form and his face told Lilly that the man definitely approved of what he saw. He definitely thought burying was a shame.

She blushed from her buried toes up.

Their eyes met and there was a sudden, pregnant silence.

'Lilly. . .'

Hamish's voice when he spoke at last held a note of wonder. He shook his head as a man shaking off a dream. 'I'd forgotten just how beautiful you were. . . how beautiful you are. . .'

'Hamish, burying is really hard work,' Davey said reprovingly, hauling Hamish's attention back to important matters and ignoring the fact that his mother's face was burning bright crimson.

Hamish appeared to give himself a mental shake. He tore his eyes from Lilly's confused gaze—and somehow managed to oblige.

He gave Lilly a lopsided grin and moved to kneel beside Davey, clearly bringing his attention back to Davey's burying with an effort.

'It seems a bit of a shame,' he said slowly. 'Burying your mum. But I guess burying people is a reasonable sort of occupation for such a fine morning. I guess I'm available for assistance if required.'

Davey considered this most generous offer. He looked down at his handiwork and then shook his head.

'Edward and I can bury her by ourselves,' he said firmly. 'You just make her lie still.'

'I will, that,' Hamish smiled and he looked back down into Lilly's face.

His smile died.

There was so much between them. So many ghosts.

'Lilly. . .'

'I. . .' Lilly faltered, and she knew her colour was refusing to fade. She brought up her arm and looked at her wristwatch. 'It's. . .it's time we were getting back,' she managed. For the life of her it was all she could think of to say.

'Mrs Price knows where we are,' Hamish told her. 'Breakfast's in an hour. There's no hurry.' He eased himself down on his towel beside her. 'You know, if you keep wearing your watch on the beach you'll ruin it,' he said conversationally.

'It's waterproof,' Lilly muttered. 'To forty fathoms or some such.'

'Forty fathoms of sand?' Hamish asked politely. 'How deep does Davey intend burying you?'

Silence.

'Lilly, we're going to have to talk,' Hamish said gently. He looked down to where Davey and Edward were involved in a deep conversation about the technicalities of leg burying. The child was clearly uninterested in adult conversation.

'What. . .what about?' It was a crazy question. Lilly knew exactly what Hamish Campbell wanted to talk about. He wanted to talk about the miniature version of Hamish Campbell playing in the sand at her feet.

'Well, for a start,' Hamish said slowly, 'can I ask exactly when Davey Campbell Inger was born?'

Lilly closed her eyes again. The nightmare was all around her and there was no way out.

'The twenty-third of November, 1991.' Her voice was flat and devoid of any emotion. This had had to happen. Some time. . . .

She waited. There was no reason to open her eyes. Hamish could do his sums all by himself.

His sums told Hamish the absolute truth. She'd been with Hamish nearly all the previous February—the February of 1991. For three magic weeks. . .

There was no denying that Hamish was Davey's father.

'Why didn't you tell me?' Hamish said at last.

'Oh, sure.' Lilly screwed her eyes even tighter closed. She didn't want to see this man. She didn't want anything to do with him. All she wanted was for the nightmare to end. 'Sure,' she repeated. 'I should have done that. I should have popped in one night and let you and your wife know you were expecting an addition to the family. How welcome would that have been?'

'But Lilly. . . Hell. . .' Hamish shook his head. 'You must have known—or suspected—almost immediately. . .'

'Oh, I suspected,' Lilly said bitterly. 'I found out for sure the day Lauris came back.'

Lauris. Lauris Campbell. Svelte, sophisticated and irrevocably married to Hamish. She'd arrived back from holiday and had been in the kitchen of Hamish's hospital flat when Lilly returned from evening ward round. Hamish had been detained at a surgical meeting and Lilly had gone back to his flat to wait for him. His bachelor flat, so she thought. . .

'So you're Hamish's little student, are you, sweetheart?' Lauris had drawled to Lilly, her cat eyes raking Lilly from head to foot as she hauled her expensive suitcase in the door and dumped it on the living-room floor. 'Have you and my husband been having fun? Well, I guess I should have expected it. When the cat's away. . .'

'So you did meet Lauris in person? And that's why you took off. . .' Hamish grimaced. 'I'd give a lot to know what she told you.'

Lilly hauled her thoughts back to the present with a jolt. Hamish was looking at her as if he really expected her to tell him the gist of that awful conversation.

She didn't even want to think about it, much less talk about it.

'It doesn't matter,' Lilly said wearily. 'Even if I hadn't been pregnant, would you really have expected me to stay? You had a great time with your student. The silly girl fell madly in love with you—so stupidly in love she didn't take the proper precautions. She was mad enough to believe the criminal lie you told her about not being able to father children.

'And then your wife comes back from her summer vacation and your nice little idyll ends. Your life takes off on its own course again—successful surgeon with beautiful wife—and I'm left with nothing.'

'Nothing?'

Lilly's eyes flew open then. 'Except Davey,' she said firmly. Her voice softened despite her anger. 'I'm left with Davey. And, despite the way you treated me, Hamish Campbell, I don't regret that.'

Davey's attention had been distracted from his burial intentions. He'd dug a small gutter around Lilly's toes and now he was wandering down to the shallows with his bucket in one hand and Edward firmly gripped in the other. He was intent on bringing sea water up to fill his channel.

The fact that the water soaked in as soon as he emptied his bucket didn't appear to worry Davey. He had the look of a child with the whole day at his disposal.

Hamish was watching Davey, too, the expression on his face unreadable.

'You didn't think of terminating the pregnancy?' Hamish asked softly, and Lilly's green eyes flashed anger.

'No.'

'Or having him adopted?'

'The easy way out?' Slowly, so as not to redisturb Davey's handiwork, Lilly pushed herself to a sitting position and stared bleakly out to sea. 'I face up to my responsibilities, Dr Campbell.'

'As opposed to me. . .?' he asked softly. The inference in Lilly's voice had been as clear as day.

'If you like.'

Hamish was silent for a moment, both man and woman watching the industrious child. The similarity between father and son was remarkable, Lilly thought bitterly. She must have been bypassed in the gene pool. It was as if Hamish had been cloned.

Davey might look like him but Hamish had no other right to the child, Lilly told herself savagely. No other right at all!

'How did you manage?' Hamish was asking, and Lilly had to force her angry mind to think.

'Manage?'

'When Davey was born.'

'Oh.' Lilly shrugged. 'I just did,' she said flatly. 'I was lucky in that Davey was born the week after my final exams. I don't. . .I don't have a family but the Salvation Army were really, really good. They looked after us for the months after Davey was born and then after I did my internship I went back and worked for their medical service as part payment. Without them, well, maybe I would have lost Davey. Or have had to give up medicine.'

'You would have given up medicine for Davey?'

'If the choice was that or giving him up.'

'I see.' Hamish's mouth was a set, grim line. 'So my son. . .my little boy. . .and his mother were cared for by welfare agencies. . .'

'I wasn't exactly helpless,' Lilly snapped, hearing criticism where maybe none was intended. 'But I had eclampsia and was really ill. . .'

'Bloody hell. . .' Hamish rose abruptly to his feet, anger surging. He turned to look down at her, the sun glinting on his bare torso and passion blazing out of his dark, dark eyes. 'Hell, Lilly, you don't think I had the right to know? Eclampsia. . . For heaven's sake, Lilly, you might have died. And you did your final exams the week before he was born? You faced that on your own? It was no bloody wonder you were ill. If you'd died. . .'

'I'd left instructions that you be contacted then,' Lilly said diffidently. 'For. . .for Davey's sake. . . If I was dead then there didn't seem a choice.'

'Oh, thanks very much. . .' It was a groan of disbelief.

'Davey's coming back,' Lilly warned. 'You're not to swear in front of my son.'

'Our son.'

'My son,' Lilly snapped. 'You have no rights to call him that, Hamish Campbell. You forfeited all rights solidly once and for all by lying to me. Your affair with me was deceitful from beginning to end and how you can look me in the eye now and say you would have been concerned, I don't know.

'Tell me, how concerned were you when you took a student to your bed knowing she was unprotected, telling her she had no worries—that you were unable to father children—and knowing your wife was due home any day? Huge social responsibility, I don't think!'

Hamish's anger faded. He stood standing before her, his hands on his lean hips, and the anger in his deep eyes slowly, slowly changed to bleakness.

'Lilly, there were reasons.'

'I'm sure there were,' Lilly snapped. 'You've had nearly five years to think of some really good ones to salve your conscience—if, in fact, you have a conscience. But I don't want to listen to a single one. Not one. This is a big beach. Why don't you go and swim or lie somewhere else—and leave us alone?'

'You mean. . .' Hamish's eyes never left her face and it seemed that the question he was about to ask was one of importance. 'You mean—for ever?'

'That's just what I do mean,' Lilly said bitterly. 'For ever.'

Hamish shook his head, almost as if he was trying to shake off the traces of some long-remembered nightmare.

'I'm sorry, Lilly,' he told her, his eyes moving back to his son. They rested on that flaming head and his face seemed to harden. 'It seems. . .it seems as if for years you've asked nothing of me—you've asked nothing when you should have been demanding my help financially at least. You should have asked, Lilly. But now. . . Now you're asking the one thing I can't do. I can't walk away from my son.'

'My son.'

'Our son,' Hamish said gently. 'Whether you like it or not, Lilly, Davey is part of me. The moment I saw him I knew that. He's my blood, Lilly, and you know that as well as I do. You don't need to worry, though, that I'll make any demands on you. I'm not in the market for any sort of relationship with a woman. I've been about as far down that road as I ever want to go, and I'm content enough as I am.'

His lips curved suddenly and there was a trace of a twinkle behind those dark eyes. 'However,' he added firmly, 'Davey seems irrevocably attached to one Edward Bear and wherever Edward goes I follow. I made that promise to Edward when I was two years old, and that promise now means I need to keep in contact with my son.'

The twinkle died as quickly as it had appeared, and Hamish stayed looking down at Lilly for a long, long moment.

'Whatever else you may think of me, Lilly Inger,' he said gently but there was iron in the soft voice, 'no matter what sort of bastard you may believe me, you have to know that I'm a man who always keeps his promises.'

Hamish let Lilly be after that, but he joined Davey, finally persuading the little boy that the best moat could be built down at the water's edge.

'Edward needs a castle fitting for a bear of distinction,' he told Davey solemnly. 'One with turrets and battlements and a throne room, and one huge vault to keep all his fabulous wealth he captured from pirates. Has Edward ever told you of his sea battles? No? I'll tell you about them while we build and Edward can sit and watch and correct me if I make any mistakes.

'It's a very long story—and just à tiny bit blood-thirsty. You don't mind the odd toenail in your stories, do you, Davey?'

Father and son moved off, Edward in tow, and started construction of an edifice which threatened to take a week at least.

Lilly watched the pair of flaming heads bent together,

listened to Davey's chuckles mixed with Hamish's rich, deep laughter and felt her world shift sideways.

No wonder she'd never contacted this man. No wonder. . . When all he had to do was be on the same beach as she was and her heart did the same sort of stupid somersaults as it had five years ago.

There was no joy down that road. No joy at all. What had Hamish said? 'I'm not in the market for any sort of relationship with a woman. I've been about as far down that road as I ever want to go. . .'

Somehow Lilly had to feel the same.

She did, she told herself savagely. There was no way she wanted to get involved again with Hamish Campbell. If only. . . If only he didn't make her feel so darned. . .so darned vulnerable.

So exposed around the heart.

Sleeping in the sun had lost its appeal. Lilly walked down to the water's edge, carefully avoiding the construction engineers and Edward near the water's edge, and launched herself into the crystal-clear surf as she tried to drive away fears, heartaches and assorted demons.

The demons refused to be driven away. After half an hour's swimming with the confusion round her heart growing rather than fading, Lilly gave up the attempt. She swam slowly back to shore to find Davey and Hamish splashing in the shallows and Davey crowing with delight.

'Hamish is going to teach me to swim,' Davey chortled. 'He says if I get out of bed early every morning he'll bring Edward and me to the beach and teach me dead-man's-float and belly-whackers and lots of other stuff. And he'll tell me all of Edward's pirate stories. Edward's a very exciting bear, really. But Hamish says I can only come if you say it's OK. It is OK, isn't it? Please, Mummy. . . Please. . .'

Lilly looked at the pleading child. Davey had been swinging from Hamish's arms and now the child was held securely against his father's chest, one small body against a very large one.

It was as if he belonged.

Like it or not, Lilly realised, this man was Davey's father. Sure he'd forfeited rights, but Davey had a right to know him. One day. . . One day she would have to tell him. . .

The thought made her cringe.

'I'm sure it's very kind of Dr Campbell,' she said stiffly and Davey gave a giggle of protest.

'He's not Dr Campbell, Mummy,' he said patiently. 'Hamish told me not to call him that. He's only Dr Campbell to patients who want too many house calls and don't take their pills on time. He says Dr Campbell makes him think of work and I make him think of nice stuff like piggybacks and sand castles and stories. So to us he's Hamish.'

So there! Hamish's grin told her, and Lilly flushed crimson.

'OK, then, Davey and. . .and Hamish. . .' Once more Lilly reverted to the protection of her watch and this time it was useful. 'It's eight o'clock. Breakfast-time. And worktime.' Hamish was setting Davey back on his feet in the shallow water and Lilly held out a hand for Davey to take. 'Come on, Davey.'

Davey shook his head. He reached up and took Hamish's hand in his—his new hero. 'I'll walk home with Hamish,' he announced. 'But you can hold my other hand, Mummy.'

'Gee, thanks,' Lilly said stiffly and tried to ignore the teasing smile lurking on Hamish Campbell's face. 'But you need to use your other hand to carry Edward— and I need to carry your bucket and spade and water-wings.'

'Remind us to bring a wheelbarrow tomorrow morning,' Hamish smiled and Davey crowed in delight.

'Let's! Let's!' he squealed. 'Tomorrow, tomorrow

and tomorrow. . . Millions and millions of tomorrows, Mummy, and all of them with Hamish.'

Oh, help. . .

CHAPTER FIVE

BREAKFAST was more than ready by the time Lilly showered both herself and Davey. Lilly ushered her small son down to the kitchen to find Mrs Price presiding over the stove and waiting for them with good-humoured patience.

'Well, well,' she beamed. 'If it's not the two water babies.'

'I'm going to learn belly-whackers, Mrs Price,' Davey announced importantly, and Mrs Price beamed.

'Dr Hamish has been telling me.' She smiled down at Lilly as Lilly sat herself down at the table. 'Isn't that just lovely?'

No, it is not, Lilly thought bitterly, but she couldn't say it.

There was a vast mound of pancakes coming out of the warming oven, and Davey's eyes grew enormous.

'Are they all for us?'

'No way.' It was Hamish's deep voice sounding from the door. Hamish took three fast steps to the table, seized the stack of pancakes and placed it firmly in front of him as he sat down. 'These are all mine, aren't they, Mrs Price?' he demanded. 'Visitors have to make do with cornflakes.'

Like Lilly and Davey, Hamish had showered and changed. He was now dressed for work. His trousers and shirt were loosely covered with his white coat and a stethoscope hung from his breast pocket, in readiness for the morning's surgery.

Davey's face fell about a foot as his pancakes disappeared—and Hamish chuckled and relented. 'Well, perhaps you can have just six,' he conceded grudgingly, handing them over. 'And your mum can have eight because she carried the water-wings all the way back from the beach. Mrs Price, how on earth are we ever going to eat all these?'

'You've been swimming. I knew you'd all be hungry and they're nice cold for elevenses,' Mrs Price said serenely. 'Dr Angus likes them cold.' She smiled down at Hamish. 'Speaking of Dr Angus. . .'

'I know.' Hamish grinned up at her and lifted the coffee-pot almost as a celebratory salute. 'I've just been up to examine him and I can't believe what I'm seeing. He's looking a hundred per cent. His colour's good. His pulse rate is down and I gather he's already eaten three pancakes. Dr Angus McVie is feeling chirpy as a spring chicken.'

Hamish looked speculatively over at Lilly. 'Could it be our Dr McVie's been under a bit of pressure? Making plans he wasn't too sure would go the right way? He looked yesterday like he was waiting for the world to collapse round his ears and I thought he was frightened of another coronary. Now I'm starting to think he was just frightened of one slip of a girl. . .'

Hamish was smiling at her and Lilly badly wanted to smile back. Badly. . .

She had lost herself in that smile once before. With a supreme effort she stopped the sides of her mouth from curving upward. 'Maybe. . .maybe he had reason to be frightened,' Lilly said darkly. 'Conniving, scheming. . .'

'That's our Dr McVie,' Hamish said cheerfully, ignoring Lilly's refusal to smile and tucking into a large serving of pancakes. 'Now he's gained his wicked way he's happy. . .'

'He hasn't gained his wicked way at all,' Lucy snapped. 'I'll stay two weeks to give you time to find someone else, Dr Campbell. Then we're leaving.'

'But, Mummy. . .' Davey broke off from his careful pouring of maple syrup and his small face crumpled in

dismay. 'I thought you said we were staying for months
and months and maybe for ever. . .'

'I know.' Lilly pushed her pancake plate back, suddenly no longer hungry. 'But. . .but the people who
persuaded me to come here weren't very honest, Davey.
So. . . Well, Davey, let's just enjoy our two weeks, shall
we? And then we'll go home.'

'Back to Sydney?' Davey wailed and Lilly bit her lip.

She didn't know. It hit her then with the force of a
sledgehammer.

The practice in Sydney no longer needed her. They'd
found another partner.

She had no money to buy into another practice.

It was locum work or nothing for a while, she decided
bleakly, moving from one practice to another and filling
in for doctors on leave.

Like it or not, after this job Lilly and her small son
had no home to go to.

The remainder of breakfast was eaten almost in
silence. Davey's misery affected them all. He munched
his pancakes with the air of a child whose world was
ending and he was just stoking up on pancakes in case
provisions were light in the hereafter.

After coffee, Lilly rose and started to clear the table.

'There's no need for you to do that,' Mrs Price told
her soundly. 'You ask Dr Hamish what needs doing if
you want to help anyone.'

Lilly sighed. She was here for two weeks to work
with Hamish Campbell as his medical partner so the
least she had to do was ask Hamish what needed doing.

'Well?' she asked, slowly turning to face him.

'Graciously put.' He smiled at her then, and there
was a trace of strain around his eyes as well. For the
first time Lilly thought that maybe he wasn't finding
this any easier than she was.

'I'm. . .I'm sorry,' she faltered. 'Just. . .just tell me
what needs doing—please—and of course I'll do it.

That's what I'm here for, and of course I intend to work.'

Their eyes locked. There was dead silence at the table.

The strain between them must be as clear as day to any onlooker, Lilly thought grimly as she finally lowered her gaze.

Thankfully, the phone on the side table rang just then and Hamish crossed to answer it with a speed that said that he was as relieved as she for the break in the conversation.

Two minutes later Hamish replaced the receiver and turned back to her.

'That was a call from the hospital in Brisbane,' he told Lilly. 'It was Ray Mark, the physician in charge of infectious diseases.'

'And?'

Lilly's eyes creased in anxiety, her thoughts flying from her personal conflict to the suffering of the little boy she'd assisted Hamish to operate on yesterday—to all of them, Henry Gibbs included. 'How are they, Hamish? Tommy and Margaret Gibbs? Are they holding their own?'

'None of them seems in danger at the moment,' Hamish reassured her. 'Margaret Gibbs's heart pain has settled. The two little girls and the older boy are a little worse, but opinion is that the antitoxin was administered soon enough to be effective. There's one more adult showing signs of illness but his immune status seems to be high enough to keep him from the worst, and Tommy's still breathing well. With luck...'

With luck there'll be no deaths, Lilly prayed, but she knew that it would be a long, long haul, especially for little Tommy—and a long period of adjustment for Margaret and Henry Gibbs.

'They've arranged quarantine for the others?'

'Yes. The government have moved heaven and earth to stop this thing in its tracks. Every national newspaper's carrying the story of diphtheria this morning and the scare's really on.' Hamish hesitated. 'Which leads me to the next thing. . .'

'Yes?'

'Lilly, I know you did evening surgery for me last night. To be truthful, I was so tired I was past noticing whether it was done or not. You must have found it hard when I hadn't even shown you the set-up here.'

'It was easy.' Lilly managed a smile. 'You use the College system of patient records, praise be. There were no problems except fear of diphtheria, and Mrs Price helped all she could.' She smiled across at the house-keeper. 'We make a good team.'

'Mrs Price is worth her weight in pancakes,' Hamish grinned. 'And we have a receptionist-cum-nursing sister on duty again this morning so you should have few problems.'

'You want me to do surgery again?'

'If you would. The authorities are worried about contamination at this end. They want to fly me over to the mainland for the morning and brief me on what needs to be done to make sure the infection hasn't left any pockets on the island.

'Also, the resort wants me to give them a clean bill of health they can use to advertise and reassure potential guests. To be honest, I don't know what that involves and I'd like to talk to some experts before I start giving guarantees to the resort manager.'

'And he'll be exerting pressure,' Lilly said sympathetically, memories of Oil-Head flooding back. She nodded. 'You go, then. I can manage.'

'You'll be all right on your own?' His eyes held hers for a moment more than necessary, and Lilly flushed like a teenager and turned away.

She had to achieve some kind of working relationship with this man—some kind of formality that would see her through two long weeks. Impossible task. Impossible.

Impossible or not, she had to start somewhere. She tilted her chin, turned and met his look head-on.

'Oh, yes,' Lilly said, more definitely than she intended, 'I'll be fine on my own.'

For some reason, it sounded like words of defiance.

In fact, it was difficult.

A new surgery where she wasn't familiar with equipment, and patients she'd never seen before. . . Lilly took twice as long as she would have in a familiar setting, and by two in the afternoon there were still patients waiting to be seen.

Most of them were suffering only from fear of diphtheria but there was the occasional more serious problem to deal with.

It was at times like these that it was easy to miss things, Lilly thought ruefully as the pressure mounted. It could be a mole ignored when it really should be checked, or someone who hadn't been seen for years fronting for diphtheria reassurance and needing blood-pressure checks or pap smears. Such patients might well not come to a doctor for another few years, Lilly knew, and to miss the opportunity was negligence.

As well as these problems, Lilly's work was made doubly difficult by the tendency of her mind to wander. When she should have been listening to Mr Haig's torrid account of his problems with his prostate, she found herself wondering just what Hamish was doing at this particular moment. . .and how long he'd be. . .

Stupid girl! There was no joy in thinking of Hamish Campbell. She hauled her mind back to Mr Haig's prostate with an effort. The man's operation was past history, but he was aching to describe it to her in every lurid detail. It was much more constructive to listen to prostate histories than think about Hamish Campbell, she told herself firmly, forcing a bright, sympathetic smile and another question to her lips.

Lilly ducked out of surgery a couple of times during

the morning to check on Davey, and on her last check
he was settled upstairs learning to play chess with
Angus McVie.

'I'll have him beating me in no time,' Angus growled
when Lilly demurred that her son might be disturbing
him. 'Get away, girl. I'm bored to snores and I've been
looking forward to young Davey's arrival to keep me
stirred.'

For how long had the old doctor been looking forward
to Davey's arrival? Lilly wondered. She looked into
Angus McVie's eyes and saw nothing but innocent com-
posure—but there was the suspicion of a twinkle that
told Lilly strongly she'd been set up by this man, and
he was quite enjoying her discomfiture. He was
certainly still hopeful of gaining his ends.

If he wasn't ill she'd throw something at him, she
thought bitterly—and then was hit by a really, really
nasty suspicion.

'Did you really have another coronary three days
ago?' she asked. 'Or are you faking it to make me stay?'

Angus grinned up at her from his pillows.

'You have a nasty, suspicious mind, girl,' he grinned.
'Just because I'm recovering nicely. . .'

'And you're not just recovering because you've
figured I'm not intending to sue or throw a tantrum or
worse. . .'

'I can't imagine a lovely young lady like you doing
anything of the kind.' Dr McVie's smile faded. 'But
unfortunately I really did have a coronary. And Hamish
had to face that damned epidemic on his own. . .'

There was real feeling in the old man's voice and
Lilly accepted his words then as absolute truth. She
walked back downstairs to her waiting patients,
accepting another truth, too. Angus McVie loved
Hamish with a fierce devotion. It was in his voice and
in his old eyes.

He'd move heaven and earth for Hamish. For his
beloved nephew. . .

Like he'd moved Lilly.

It'd be lovely to have a family like that to care for you, Lilly thought sadly. Lovely. . .

All she had was Davey.

It was no use letting her thoughts run in those miserable channels. Lilly gritted her teeth and worked on, and at two in the afternoon the receptionist saw out Lilly's last seen patient and came tentatively into the room.

'Dr Inger?'

Lilly finished writing up the patient's record and looked up. The receptionist was looking worried.

'Yes?'

'I'm sorry. . .' The young woman frowned. 'It's just. . .I usually finish at one, and I've agreed to take library duty this afternoon at my daughter's school. I only do it once a month and she does look forward to it.'

Lilly sighed and managed a smile. 'How many more are there to see?'

'Five.' The receptionist smiled back. 'And I've put their histories out on the reception desk in order and there are no more booked in. The islanders know now they'll have to wait until evening clinic if they haven't booked in by now.'

'OK, then,' Lilly agreed. 'I'll manage.'

The next four patients were straightforward cases of diphtheria phobia, with one papilloma enquiry thrown in. Lilly didn't know what the situation was with the provision of liquid nitrogen so she deferred treatment of the calloused wart to a further consulation. That left one patient. Lilly saw out her second-last patient and turned to her last.

He was a young man in his early twenties. Lilly had been aware of him sitting patiently waiting, as every time she emerged to collect the next patient and matching history he'd flashed her a blinding smile. The man was tanned and good-looking, if a trifle thin, and his startlingly blue eyes were obviously accustomed to having an effect on the ladies in his immediate vicinity.

Lilly emerged to call him in and frowned. There was no history on the desk.

She looked at the booking sheet. Wayne Reid.

No history.

'Could you hold on for a moment?' She frowned and walked into the small back room where the histories were stored.

Still no history. The place in the filing cabinet where Wayne Reid's records should be stored was empty.

'Are you a new patient to the practice?' she queried, returning to Reception.

'Heck, no, lady,' he smiled. 'I'm an islander, born and bred. I've been coming here since my mum brought me here with nappy rash.'

Lilly smiled back and ushered him through, her mind uneasy. She was sure that there'd been five patient folders lying on the reception desk when the receptionist had left. She should have brought them all through into her surgery then.

Maybe it didn't matter. As long as it wasn't lost permanently. If the young man just had a sore throat. . .

He didn't. The young man settled carefully, stiffly, into the chair before her desk, smiled his enchanting smile and confessed to chronic back pain.

'I came off my surfboard a while back,' he said easily. 'Got dumped good and proper and spent weeks flat on my back. Doc Campbell sent me to the mainland to see specialists and I'm booked for an operation next month, but in the meantime I need morphine. The pain gets pretty much unbearable, especially at night. I'm all out, so I just want a repeat prescription.'

Oh, help. . .

Lilly winced. Now what? She had no patient record, no X-rays, no proof at all that what this man was saying was true—and he was asking for morphine.

He was sitting stiffly in his chair, as if he was protecting a rigid and painful back—but surely he had been lounging out in Reception with a magazine in his hands? And surely she, trained to notice such things, would have noticed it if he'd been sitting like this then.

'What exactly happened to your back?' she asked cautiously.

'I've got a herniated disc,' he told her. 'Third vertebra. Local swelling's gone now, because we're looking at a six-month history but it still gives me hell. Runs into my neck and there's sciatica in my leg too. Insomnia. Headaches. You name it. Plays hell with my social life, I can tell you.'

'I'm sure it must.' Lilly drummed her fingers on the desk. 'Are you employed, Mr Reid?'

'I work on my dad's fishing boat,' the man told her. 'At least, I do when the pain's not too bad. I can manage it—as long as I have the morphine. . .'

Lilly looked across at the man's hands and the faint warning bells grew louder. Those weren't fisherman's hands. Those hands looked like they'd never seen a hard day's work in their lives.

'Well, let's have a look at your back, then,' she said easily. 'Could you take your shirt off, please?'

'Heck, do we have to do this?' the man demanded. 'My problems are all in the notes. Or Dr Campbell knows about it. Just ask him.'

'Dr Campbell's on the mainland today,' Lilly said and saw just a tiny flicker of something that might have been triumph in the man's eyes.

It was as if he'd planned it. Lilly thought fast, her worry increasing by the second. Every islander worth his salt could find out that Dr Campbell was on the mainland today, and a new doctor might seem like a soft touch.

'Mr Reid, you're asking me to prescribe a strong narcotic,' Lilly said slowly. 'I'm sorry, but I have to examine you. . .'

She met her young patient's eyes and was startled

by the anger she saw there. His easy charm was slipping fast.

'Look, just because your surgery's so damned inept it loses its patient records. . .' The good humour had disappeared completely and the blue eyes flashed icily. It was as much as Lilly could do not to recoil.

'Mr Reid, you've no doubt heard of the diphtheria epidemic,' Lilly managed to say, keeping her grip on her calmness with an effort. 'I just arrived on the island yesterday and I'm very new. OK, I can't find your history but you're going to have to humour me, please. I can't prescribe what you want without an examination. I'll be fast, and I'll be gentle. But I do need to examine you. . .'

The anger slowly faded. The blue eyes looked at her speculatively and the eyes grew frankly appraising. Lilly didn't enjoy his look one bit. It was as if his eyes were looking underneath the white coat and serviceable dress. He liked what he saw, his look told her, and inwardly Lilly's anger mounted.

'Well, seeing it's you,' the man smiled finally. The smile was just a bit too suggestive. 'And as long as your hands are warm.'

Lilly found absolutely no clinical signs of a herniated disc at all.

Sure, there were reactions of pain—but the reactions were worrying. There was no consistency. One place hurt and then, after careful checks elsewhere, the pain centres seemed to shift upward. Or downward. . .

'Do you get your scripts filled here or on the mainland?' Lilly asked as she finally allowed him to dress. She crossed to her desk and lifted her pen, and once more there was that flicker of triumph in the blue, blue eyes. Lilly pulled a script pad toward her and saw the triumph deepen.

'On the mainland,' the man assured her easily. 'They don't keep enough of the stuff here. Though. . .' He frowned. 'I know the doctors here keep a bit on stock

in the clinic for emergency use—and I won't be able
to get to the mainland until tomorrow. Do you reckon
you could let me have enough to tide me over, as well
as the prescription?'

'I'll have to check. . .' It was the opening Lilly had
been looking for. She smiled apologetically at him. 'I
really don't know what we have in stock and what we
don't. If you'll stay here for a moment, I'll see. . .'

She glanced casually at her blank prescription pad
and then rose. 'I'll just be a moment.'

One minute later she was in Angus McVie's bedroom.
The old man was propped up on pillows looking out
over the garden. The chess game was obviously over.
Angus looked up and smiled as Lilly knocked and
entered, and Lilly saw that he'd been watching Davey
playing down in the garden.

His smile faded when he saw Lilly's face.

'What is it, lass?' His old eyes searched hers, sensing
trouble.

'Wayne Reid. . .'

She hadn't missed her bet. Angus McVie's face
closed in anger.

'Hell, girl, has that no-good layabout been
bothering you?'

As Lilly outlined what was happening, Angus's face
grew thunderous. 'Sneaking, rotten little creep he is. . .'
He lay back against the white linen and Lilly winced.
Maybe she shouldn't have bothered Angus with this.
Angus saw her look, though, and shook her head.

'You needn't worry, lass. I refuse to have another
coronary on that one's account. But I'll come down and
see him off the premises. . .'

'You will not,' Lilly said, alarmed. 'Dr McVie, I
didn't come up here to ask for your physical help. I
just want to know who he is.'

'He's a drug-pusher, that's what he is,' Angus
growled. 'Well, he has been a drug-pusher. The rumour

is he's too well known now to get supplies any more and he's also picked up a habit himself.'

'He's an islander?' Lilly asked and Angus shook his head.

'No way. But our Mr Reid keeps tabs on all the mainland doctors, as well as the doctors on the nearby islands, and he knows when a new doctor or locum arrives. He'll have known I was ill and you were arriving.

'When Hamish went to the mainland today the creep will've rung up for an appointment immediately and come over with the return ferry. Just to try you out. I guess he couldn't believe his luck when his history was on the desk. Heaven knows how he got rid of it.'

'Why didn't he book under a false name?' Lilly asked curiously.

Angus shook his head. 'If he's become addicted himself then money will be tight—and if he uses a false name he can't use his health card. He's probably banking on the thought that new doctors can be bulldozed regardless. It's often easier to give them what they want than to argue.' Angus pushed back his bedcovers. 'Go on, girl. Give me a hand downstairs and I'll give him his marching orders.'

How threatening would one weak, pyjama-clad old doctor be? Lilly thought wryly, but she didn't say it. Instead, she pulled the bedclothes up firmly again and tucked him in.

'Dr McVie, you just keep supervising Davey,' she said severely, motioning down to the child in the garden. 'I haven't been a medical officer for welfare agencies without learning how to deal with drug addicts.'

It wasn't quite true.

Lilly's usual policy in her Sydney surgery had been to hit the alarm button under her desk, which meant that her normal receptionist had been speedily replaced by a burly security guard who'd just happened to open the door and ask if things were fine.

There was no security guard here—and there was the thought of just enough anger behind Wayne Reid's blue eyes to make Lilly lift the phone and dial the police station before she returned to the surgery.

The policeman's wife answered.

'The sergeant's out over at the resort,' the woman told her pleasantly. 'The mainland health authorities are on the island—they arrived by helicopter half an hour ago—and they're telling my husband what needs to be done with the quarantined part of the resort. I can contact him if it's urgent.'

Lilly hesitated. If the health authorities were at the resort then Hamish would be probably be there too. A call would have both policeman and Hamish tearing back, and she'd seem like a helpless, female wimp.

And she badly didn't want to appear a wimp before Hamish.

There was a small part—or maybe it was a very large part—of her that was telling her very firmly to try and contact Hamish, but that was the part of her that she'd fought so strongly for nearly five years.

She did not need Hamish Campbell!

It was just an addict asking for a script, after all. Surely she should cope.

'Of course you can, Lilly Inger,' she told herself harshly. 'I don't need any policeman—or Hamish Campbell either, for that matter. You're a big girl now and you're making a mountain out of a molehill.'

She looked over at the door through to the surgery at the side of the house, took a deep breath and went back in to face her molehill.

Or her mountain. . .

CHAPTER SIX

WAYNE REID was still waiting. The young man sat with his arms folded, outwardly calm but his foot tapping the floor with an odd, erratic rhythm. He looked up as Lilly entered and his eyes searched her empty hands.

'You didn't bring it, then?' There was strain in his voice.

'There's none here,' Lilly lied, sitting down again at her chair on the far side of the desk. 'I'd imagine Dr Campbell must be restocking while he's over on the mainland.'

The desire for Hamish's presence was still right there—seemingly overwhelming. She shoved the wish away hard. Concentrate on Wayne Reid...

The man was grimacing as though in pain. Now he leaned over the desk and practically shoved Lilly's prescription pad at her. 'Well, fill this in for me,' he snapped.

Lilly glanced down, and then looked again harder at her pad of blank prescriptions. The number on the top script was ten numbers further on than the script she'd seen as she'd left.

The scripts were issued in numerical sequence. She'd made no mistake. Wayne Reid must now have ten stolen blank prescription forms somewhere in his pockets.

He'd want a script from her anyway, she knew. A legitimate script couldn't be questioned by a pharmacist but if push came to shove he'd write his stolen scripts for morphine—or any drug he liked, if it came to that—and try to persuade a pharmacist that she'd written them.

She was a new doctor in the district. No local pharmacist knew Lilly's handwriting yet. This man would probably succeed in having his stolen scripts filled.

Lilly took a deep breath. OK, Lilly, she told herself.
So your molehill is growing. Well, all you can do now
is face your mountain with calm.

'Mr Reid, maybe you know our senior partner, Dr
McVie, is ill,' Lilly said steadily. 'He's convalescing
here. While I was out of the room I asked him what he
knew of your back problems.'

The blue eyes froze. The foot stopped its tapping.

'Maybe you can guess what Dr McVie told me,' Lilly
continued, meeting those blank eyes fair and square.
'Mr Reid, you must know I can't give you morphine—
though I can help you in other ways.'

'Yeah?' Still those eyes were blank.

'You have a problem, I gather,' Lilly said gently.
'And I'd like to help—if you'll let me.' She took
another deep breath. 'But first. . . First I think you
should give me back my blank prescriptions.'

The blankness faded then. The man rose to his feet
and the look in his eyes changed to one where Lilly
would have given quite a lot—any amount really—to
have a security button at hand.

Or Hamish. Hamish. . .

'Make me,' the man whispered.

'You know I can't do that either.' Lilly's voice was
miles steadier than she felt, but somehow she main-
tained outward calm. 'But I can contact the police after
you've gone and the only way you can return to the
mainland is via the ferry—or charter boat, if you can
afford it. But I don't think you can afford a charter
boat, can you, Mr Reid?'

She held out her hand. 'The police can pick you up
on the ferry, so maybe. . . Maybe you should just give
me the scripts and we'll forget I ever noticed they were
missing.'

Things were starting to go wrong here. She had
misjudged her man. Seriously.

Lilly had thought that Wayne Reid had himself under
control and could still think logically. She had thought

that he was a man on the edge of addiction, who could face failure and accept it without doing something stupid.

There was no longer any control here, though. Something awful could happen soon. The look in Wayne Reid's blue eyes was one of thwarted fury.

His arm rose.

Lilly moved fast backward, but not fast enough. Wayne Reid leaned forward over the desk and his hand caught her hard across the face in a savage blow that threw her back against the wall.

'Bitch!' the man snarled, moving like a vengeful predator round to her side of the desk. 'Bitch-face! What gives you the right to tell me what I can and can't have? You two-faced, lying little. . .'

He was advancing as he spoke, his hand raised, but this time his fist was clenched. Lilly threw herself sideways but she couldn't avoid what was coming. The fist caught her coming down, driving into her shoulder so hard that she almost cried out in pain.

Almost. Somehow, though, she bit the sound back.

There were two crises here. This man was intending to hurt her—but surely he would stop short of murder. And if she cried out. . . If she cried out then Mrs Price and Angus McVie would hear and Lilly knew for sure what that would mean. She had no doubt that Angus McVie would be down here in a flash, his blood pressure racing.

It would probably kill him.

So. . . She'd been a fool to think that she could cope alone and she was facing the consequences—but Angus McVie couldn't face them for her.

She was alone. And she had to force herself to think.

Her attacker's hand was rising again. She was half crouched before him, her head level with his chest. Her knees were sagging, bending upward as she cringed back. . .

Some time ago, in her student days, Lilly had done

a self-defence course for women. One night of basic techniques, long forgotten. . .

Not quite. Something stirred so fleetingly that her movement to self-defence was almost instinct rather than thought.

Lilly's knee jabbed up hard, so hard that she almost fell off balance. The hard centre of her knee smashed with all her force just where she intended—just where she'd been taught a male assailant would feel it most. The impact was sickening.

The man's eyes widened with incredulous pain but before he could react Lilly had steadied herself and straightened. Her hands came round the man's neck— upward, gripping his hair. His head was dragged down before he had time to pull back and her knee once more jerked up, this time smashing hard into his jaw.

She heard it crack. . .

Her hands fell back in a nerveless reaction of fear. What had she done?

The man's hands were clutching his groin. Now he took two staggering steps backward and his hands lifted away to touch his wounded face. There was blood starting to trickle down his jaw.

There was blood somewhere on Lilly's face, too. She could feel it running warmly down. It seemed the least of her worries.

'You. . .you bitch. . .'

Lilly felt rather than saw him gather strength. Dear heaven, there was only one way this could end. She had hurt him twice but only because she'd caught him by surprise, and the injuries she'd inflicted had only been intended—taught by her self-defence instructor— to give a victim a chance to run.

Here there was nowhere to run. The man was between Lilly and the door. He was much larger—much stronger—and he didn't care one whit who he hurt. . .

He was coming for her again.

No!

She put her hands up uselessly to deflect the blow, knowing that there was no way she could stop the pain now and inside her head a silent scream was echoing over and over.

No! Please. . .

And somehow her plea worked.

Suddenly—miraculously—her attacker was no longer lunging over her. One second the hand was raised to strike, and the next the man was being hauled away by some unknown force.

Lilly stared up in stunned amazement as Wayne Reid fell backward—and then her appalled gaze shifted to find the force propelling him backward across the room.

Hamish! It was Hamish. Hamish Campbell had entered in silence, and now he was hauling Wayne Reid back from her with the strength of ten men.

How he did it she couldn't tell, but there was no doubt that Hamish knew what he was about. In one swift, savage movement her assailant was locked with his face pressed hard against the opposite wall. His arms were hauled up behind his back in a grip that was painful even to see.

'You move and I'll break both your arms,' Hamish threatened in a voice that was laced with ice. 'Lilly. . . Lilly, are you OK?' Hamish didn't look back at her. His attention was all on the drug addict he was gripping in fury.

Lilly hadn't moved. Now she slowly uncurled from her crouched position. She must have cringed back again, she realised, though she couldn't remember doing it.

She stared at Hamish and the man who'd attacked her in stunned silence.

The danger was over. The combination of the damage Lilly had done and Hamish's strong and painful hold had robbed Wayne Reid of all his courage. Now he snivelled into the wall.

'You've busted my teeth,' he whined. 'Let me go.

You bastards, I can feel busted teeth. I'll sue. . .I'll sue. . .'

'Ring the police, Lilly,' Hamish told her, not looking back to see if she obeyed. He didn't take his eyes from the man in his hold. 'The sergeant just dropped me off here so he should just about be home by now.'

'Shouldn't. . .shouldn't we check him f-first?' Lilly asked shakily as she tried to make her legs carry her to the phone. Her lower limbs felt like jelly. 'I mean. . .I think I might. . .I might have hurt him.'

'I hope you did—but I'm sure you didn't hurt him hard enough,' Hamish growled. 'He's not at death's door so, no, I don't think we should examine him.' Hamish gave Wayne another shove as the man tried to writhe free. 'This creep's up on an assault charge at the very least and if I let him go he won't stick round to face it. I'm not moving until the police arrive.' He hauled Wayne Reid's arms higher in his locking hold, stopping the last of his efforts to free himself. 'And neither are you, Reid. . .'

It was the longest five minutes Lilly had ever spent. No one spoke. All Lilly could hear was the heavy breathing of the two men. Hamish must have been running before he'd entered the surgery, Lilly thought. And Wayne Reid. . . The man was snivelling and panting and groaning, but he wasn't speaking.

There was nothing to say.

Finally they heard the police car draw up outside and heavy footsteps running along the path. Lilly moved stiffly to let the policeman in.

'What the. . .?'

The policeman got no further. The policeman's eyes moved quickly round the surgery and his handcuffs were out before he finished the sentence.

This policeman was no fool. He summed the situation up in seconds and in even less time Hamish was rid of his responsibility. Wayne Reid was handcuffed and helpless.

'Now, would someone like to tell me what's going on?' the policeman demanded as he clicked the handcuffs locked. He glanced round all their faces as he took control of the addict, and his mouth tightened as his eyes finally rested on his prisoner. 'Not that I can't guess.'

'There'll be some of my prescription forms in his pockets,' Lilly said wearily. 'He stole them.'

'Bitch,' Reid snarled, his voice so menacing that Lilly flinched, and all at once Hamish's arm was around her, supporting her, holding her against him in a grip of iron.

She didn't resist. She couldn't. Lilly couldn't help herself. She found herself sagging against Hamish's body and, without his strength, she would have fallen.

'I'll bloody lay an assault charge against you,' Reid snarled. He wiped a trickle of blood from his lip. 'I just asked for a script and the bloody bitch went for me. . .'

'Planted script forms in your pockets too, I'll bet,' the policeman said evenly. 'You save your story for the judge.' He looked closely at Lilly. 'Are you OK, miss? I mean—Doctor?'

'No, she's not OK.' Hamish's grip tightened even further around her waist. Lilly was shaking like a leaf and he could feel the tremors through her thin cotton dress and white coat. 'Sergeant, if you'd like to take this creep out of here we'll come down to the station later and make a statement.'

His eyes gave the policeman an urgent message and the policeman nodded.

'Fine by me, Doc.' He gave Wayne a shove toward the door. 'Let's go, mate.'

'What are you going to do about my bloody face?' the man screamed. 'The bitch broke my teeth. I can feel them. If you don't give me something for the pain. . .'

The policeman looked back at Hamish and the sergeant's mouth twitched.

'I don't reckon you'll get a lot of sympathy for your pain here, mate,' the policeman said easily. 'I reckon we might ship you over to the mainland on the police launch. There'll be a doctor over at the main lock-up who'll know what you need.'

He shoved the man out, and they heard Wayne Reid snivelling all the way to the police car.

Silence.

Lilly's legs had given way beneath her and if Hamish hadn't been holding her she would have crumpled where she stood. Hamish half led, half carried her to a chair and propelled her into it.

'Let's see what the damage is, shall we, Lilly?' His voice was laced with tenderness and caring, and it was all Lilly could do not to burst into tears.

'I'm not. . .' she tried to say and her voice was a shaken whisper. Hamish had his fingers under her chin, forcing her face up so that he could see why she was bleeding, and she tried feebly to push his hand away. 'I don't need. . . Please. . . I'll be all right.'

'You can cope alone, can you, Lilly?' Hamish asked, and the tenderness hadn't abated one bit. 'Little fool. . .'

'I'm not. . .I'm not a fool.'

'So, when did you ever learn you could face drug addicts alone?'

'I didn't. . .' It was so hard to get her voice to work. 'I didn't think he was so far out of control. . . I'm not stupid. But if I'd called for help. . .'

'I know. Angus would have been down here in a flash, and that creep would have had Angus's death to answer for.'

Hamish's fingers were gently examining her face as he spoke. He took a swab from the tray Sister had left prepared on a side table and started cleaning blood from her cheek. 'And it's thanks to you he doesn't.' His face tightened. 'Hell, Lilly, he must have hit you with force. He's split the skin above your ear. I'm going to have to stitch it.'

'Don't mind me,' Lilly said with a tiny flash of strained humour. Her voice sounded weird. 'I'll. . .I'll just think of England.'

He knelt down before her then, and his gaze carefully searched her eyes.

'There's more than just this blow to your face, isn't there, Lilly?'

He must have been able to hear the pain in my voice, she decided vaguely. Her mind didn't seem to be operating on any sort of normal level at all.

For a moment Lilly thought of not telling him, but she knew he'd find out anyway. This man's eyes had a habit of seeing too darned much. The pain from her shoulder was making her feel sick.

'He hit. . .he hit me on the shoulder,' she whispered. 'It hurts. . .more than my face.'

It was hurting like crazy, she thought faintly. In fact, the room was showing an alarming propensity to spin.

Hamish swore. Not a mild swear-word. On an obscenity scale of one to ten, the label Hamish applied to Wayne Reid was right up there in the big league. In fact, Lilly couldn't remember ever hearing such a word from Hamish Campbell before.

She blinked and blinked again, but then the dizziness receded as she was swept off her chair and placed prone on the examination couch.

'Lie there before you fall,' Hamish growled. Lilly's face was losing colour by the second. He pulled back her white coat and swore again as he realised that her dress zipped at the back and her coat buttoned at the front. Another oath and he had the scissors in his hand—and was cutting.

'Hamish. . .' Lilly's voice was a faint squeak. 'That's my dress. . .'

'I'll buy you another one,' Hamish said savagely. 'The bastard. The stupid, mindless, murderous bastard. . .'

He stripped back the rent fabric at Lilly's left shoulder and stared down in grim silence.

'What?' Lilly said faintly. She couldn't see. She could only feel—and what she felt was bad enough. 'What. . .?'

'You've a haematoma. There's bleeding under the skin over an area the size of a fist,' Hamish said grimly. He turned fast to the drug cupboard and loaded a syringe. 'A good, fast painkiller is called for, I believe, Dr Inger.'

'I don't want. . .'

'Remind me to ask you what you want when next I'm interested,' Hamish growled. 'Dr Inger, just shut up and let an older and wiser doctor do what needs to be done. Hear?'

Lilly looked up and met those fierce, tender eyes and for a long, long moment their eyes locked.

Nothing had changed.

Dear heaven, those eyes. . .

She couldn't refuse him. She never had been able to refuse Hamish Campbell anything.

Because she loved him.

Don't be so stupid, she told herself harshly and the combination of shock, pain and emotion brought a glimmer of tears to her eyes. The tears were blinked back fast. Get a grip on yourself. Somehow. Somehow. . .

Somehow she must.

Lilly Inger had to walk away from here at the end of two weeks with her heart somehow intact and her world still revolving round only Lilly Inger and her small son, Davey.

So save your reserves for the real fight, she thought wearily as she closed her eyes against that look. Heaven help her, she was going to need all the reserves she could muster.

'OK,' she said faintly. 'Do. . .do what you must.'

There was a long, long moment of silence.

'I always have,' Hamish said at last, and his voice was laced with bitterness, long remembered. 'I always have.'

CHAPTER SEVEN

THE rest of the day passed in a blur.

Mrs Price was told what had happened, but neither Davey nor Angus were to know. Hamish placed three careful stitches in the gash above Lilly's ear, dressed the wound carefully, placed compresses on her shoulder and then helped her up to bed.

Then, while Hamish distracted Davey, Mrs Price came in to help her undress and then bustled off importantly to make chicken soup—the lady's answer to all domestic crises, Lilly gathered.

Hamish re-entered her room the moment Mrs Price left.

'That's better,' he smiled as he saw her settled under the covers.

'It is not better.' Lilly stirred restlessly under the sheets and winced as pain knifed through her shoulder. 'Dr Campbell, I don't need to stay here.'

'And I'm saying you do,' Hamish said firmly. He crossed to pull her covers more firmly around her and his hand rested lightly on her arm. 'Lilly, you're to stay here for the rest of the day.'

'But Davey. . . And Dr McVie. . .'

'We're telling them you're over taking swabs from the employees at the resort,' he told her. 'Mrs Price kept Davey out of the way while I brought you upstairs—and then I taught Davey elementary mud pie making while Mrs Price undressed you.' He smiled down at her with a smile that nudged Lilly close to tears. It was a caress in itself, undermining all her fragile defences.

'In some ways, Lilly Inger, I'm finding my son's education sadly lacking,' Hamish smiled softly. 'To reach his fourth birthday without learning the rudiments of making a decent mud pie. . .'

Lilly managed a smile in return and Hamish couldn't have known what the effort cost her.

'I'm. . .I'm sorry. . .'

'Oh, for heaven's sake. . .' Hamish's smile slipped and he touched her face lightly with his hand. 'I was joking,' he said softly. 'Don't be sorry—even for an instant. Davey's a great little kid, Lilly.'

'I. . .I know.' She couldn't help it. A single tear slid down her cheek and Hamish swore gently and wiped it away.

'You're knocked to pieces, Lilly Inger.' His voice was gentle but then it changed. 'Bastard. . .I shouldn't have left you alone.' He grimaced, his mouth set, and Lilly knew that he was thinking very uncharitable thoughts about drug addicts. Very uncharitable. . .

She winced. It was such a strange feeling to have someone angry on her behalf. Weird. . .

Addictive in itself.

'I have to get up,' she made herself say. 'I must. . . Davey. . .'

'Davey will be busy with his mud pies for hours yet,' Hamish said firmly in a voice that brooked no argument. 'Mrs Price and I have decided you'll slip on a soapy floor while you're over at the resort—some time about now—and graze your face. That'll explain away your bandage. As well as Davey, Angus would be really upset and blame himself if he knew what had happened and I know you don't want that.'

Hamish hesitated then as if not sure what to say next. His gaze didn't leave her face. He stood beside the bed, looking down at Lilly's pale, battered face, and his eyes held a mixture of tenderness and wonder.

Hamish had tried to carry her upstairs but Lilly had thwarted him by threatening to scream blue murder if he lifted her. She'd walked, with Hamish so close that she couldn't have fallen if she'd tried. Now he looked down at this pale slip of a girl and he shook his head in confusion.

'You might threaten to scream when you don't wish to do what I say, Dr Lillian Inger,' he said slowly at last, 'but how on earth did you keep your mouth closed when that oaf was hitting you?'

Lilly swallowed. 'I knew. . .I knew Angus would come if I screamed. . .'

Hamish shook his head again. The look of bewilderment deepened.

'And it's only luck that I came when I did. Marie— our receptionist—should have recognised Reid's name when she booked him. She should have warned you. She'll feel dreadful when she learns what happened. I guess she's not used to having a doctor who doesn't know the patients. . .'

'It doesn't matter. . .'

'It did matter, though,' Hamish said savagely. His frown deepened as he thought through the sequence of events. 'I must have returned to the house just after you left Angus's bedroom. I went up to see Angus and found him fretting over what was happening downstairs—so I came down to the surgery to check. But if I hadn't. . . Lilly, you realise Wayne Reid could easily have killed you? And you. . .you would have shut up and let him!'

'Maybe. . . Maybe I would have cried out if it had got much worse,' Lilly said slowly, her hand moving unconsciously to her injured shoulder.

'Maybe. . .' Hamish sank to sit on the edge of her bed and his hand came out to cover the fingers that were probing her shoulder. 'Don't touch it, Lilly. It'll make the pain worse. It's going to ache for days as it is.'

Lilly nodded and tried to let her hand fall away— but Hamish didn't let it fall. Instead, he gripped her fingers in his strong, warm clasp and held them hard.

'Lilly. . .'

She closed her eyes. There was enough confusion in Hamish's voice to make her turn from what was coming.

'Lilly, look at me.'

The pethidine he'd given her was dulling her senses. She had nothing left to fight him with—for the moment.

Wearily she obeyed him, opening her eyes and forcing herself to meet his look.

'Lilly, when did your parents die?'

If she'd expected any question it hadn't been this. She blinked, trying to focus.

'I don't. . .' She blinked again. 'I don't. . .'

'Tell me,' he said firmly. He looked down at this pale waif of a woman-child, her bright curls tumbled around the pillow and her bandaged face bereft of any colour at all. She was half-asleep and confused by the pethidine, and some instinct told Hamish that if he wanted answers to questions that troubled him now was the time to ask. She had strength, this girl. If she wanted to keep things to herself there'd be few chances to find chinks in her armour.

'Tell me, Lilly,' he said again and his hands gripped hers more tightly.

Lilly stirred and sighed. This was all so hard. It was easier to do what he said than refuse. Easier to give in. . .

'My. . .my father was never there,' she whispered slowly. 'He left before I remember. But my mum. . . my mum died when I was fifteen.'

'Do you have any relatives at all?'

It all seemed so darned inconsequential, when all Lilly wanted was to sleep. Or lie back and savour the feel of this man's hands holding hers. . .

'I had a great-aunt, but she was an invalid and she. . . she died too. So not now. Not that I know.'

'Then how on earth did you make it through medical school?'

This was easier.

'Scholarship,' she said firmly. Her voice sounded strange.

'So when you found you were pregnant. . .' For some reason Lilly was too tired to figure out there was pain in Hamish Campbell's voice. It matched the pain in her shoulder—or maybe it was worse. It strengthened the link between their hands. Pain matching pain. 'So when I made you pregnant you had absolutely no one to turn to. Except me.'

'Not to you.' It was as if it wasn't Lilly who was speaking. It was someone else. Some disembodied voice from the other side of the room. 'I couldn't turn to you. You were married.'

'Of course,' Hamish said bitterly. 'I was married. And you had to protect my marriage at all costs. Like you risked your life just then to protect Angus. . .'

'H-Hamish. . .' Suddenly this was unbearable. Lilly hauled at her hands and they were finally— reluctantly—released.

'Yes, my dear.' Hamish's voice was infinitely tender.

She wasn't his dear. She wasn't this man's anything at all.

'Hamish, I need to sleep,' she said and her voice was tight with their linked pain. 'Please. . . Please, go away.'

'Is that what you want?'

'Yes.'

He rose and stood looking down at her for a long, long moment, like a man looking down at a sweetly remembered dream.

Something that he knew would vanish again at any moment.

'If that's what you want,' he said tenderly and touched her lips with his finger. 'But I'll be back, my Lilly. I'll be back.'

Lilly remembered little more of the day. Hamish came in once or twice, but only fleetingly. Ignoring her protests, he gave her another injection toward nightfall and she drifted into a sleep where her dreams drifted from sweetness to horror.

Threats and comfort.

Wayne Reid—and Hamish Campbell.

Comfort won.

The thought of Hamish stayed with her, protecting her sleep from nightmares, and Lilly finally dreamed with a smile on her lips.

She woke just after dawn feeling a hundred per cent better. The shock had faded, leaving only dull aches with the bruising.

She lay and listened to the birds' dawn chorus mixed with the sounds of the surf, and somewhere in those sounds there was even peace for her confused mind. For her battered heart. . .

Peace and four-year-olds didn't mix, though. They never have.

Lilly smiled to herself as she heard her son stir next door just twenty minutes after first light—and then she frowned when, instead of bursting into her room, she heard Davey's small feet thudding downstairs.

From somewhere below she heard a mixture of a small boy's voice and a deep, masculine response that was all too familiar, then doors banging, voices outside and finally two sets of footsteps coming up the stairs.

Father and son appeared, both heads peering round her bedroom door one above the other. Davey seemed agog with excitement and Hamish was twinkling above him, peeping in to see whether she was awake.

They ventured further.

Both males were clad only in swimming costumes.

Lilly blinked.

And stared.

How had she ever thought that she could keep this pair apart? These two—Hamish Campbell and David Campbell Inger—were two halves of a whole. Their hands were linked now, but more than that linked them. The twinkling eyes were a matched set of four.

'Mummy, we're going swimming,' Davey announced importantly, beaming as he saw her awake. He crossed to the bed and checked out her bandage with the careful scrutiny of a four-year-old checking a treasured possession for damage. 'Hamish told me last night you'd hurt yourself and had to have a sleep-in— and he told me to wake him up first this morning.' He frowned down into her face. 'Is it really, really sore, Mummy?'

Lilly smiled and pushed herself to an upright position on her pillows. She gathered her near-naked son close in a gesture that had more to do with defence than anything else. The other near-naked figure was all too close.

'It's fine,' she smiled. 'It only hurts when I laugh. Am I invited to the beach, too?'

'Sure.' Davey wiggled in close. 'Will you swim?'

'Maybe not this morning,' Lilly told him, wincing a little as his small body nudged her shoulder. 'But I'm sure as heck not being left behind.'

If Hamish thought that she was meekly staying here while he insinuated himself into her son's affections, he had another thought coming! Then, as she glanced up at Hamish and saw the twinkle deepen, she had second thoughts.

Maybe this was what he'd planned all along. To have her come too.

'I think you might have trouble swimming.' Regardless of her suspicions, there was no trace of triumph in Hamish's deep voice and Lilly shoved her uncharitable thoughts aside for the moment.

Hamish crossed the room and lightly touched her injured shoulder, sending a shiver of sensation through her body that Lilly had trouble describing. She lifted a hand to brush his fingers aside but he was faster, withdrawing by sweeping the small Davey up into muscled arms.

'I've blown up the air-mattress so you can lie in comfort on the beach while your menfolk work,' he smiled down into her troubled eyes. 'Davey and I have put it in our wheelbarrow. This morning we're going prepared.'

'Wheelbarrow...' It was all Lilly could do to make herself say the word wheelbarrow. The words echoing round and round in her head were the ones Hamish had spoken later. 'While your menfolk work... Your menfolk...'

'We figured we needed a wheelbarrow at least,' Hamish grinned. 'Davey and I are geared for heavy construction this morning. We have two full-sized garden spades—no little plastic jobs for real men like us—two large buckets, your air mattress, Davey's water-wings, sun screen, beach towels, fruit juice— courtesy of Mrs Price—and last, but not least, we have Edward. Plus you. If your legs are a bit wobbly we can probably stack you on top.'

'Gee, thanks.' Lilly's voice was a trifle breathless and Hamish looked at her closely.

'Stay in bed if you'd like, Lilly,' he said gently. 'Davey and I are fine on our own.'

Where had she heard that phrase before?

Lilly shook her head and made herself smile.

'I'm coming,' she said definitely. Absolutely. 'Are we bringing the kitchen sink, too?'

'If you like,' Hamish said equitably. 'Mrs Price probably doesn't want to give hers up but if you've another handy then, by all means, bring it along. I think we have everything else.'

They left her to dress.

Lilly donned a simple cotton frock that hid her injured shoulder. She brushed her hair and left it hanging free to disguise most of the bandage on her face, slipped on sandals and then walked slowly downstairs.

Father and son were ready and waiting. The wheelbarrow was piled high, with Davey perched triumphantly on top of the pile holding Edward even higher and crowing with delight.

'We're going to the beach! We're going to the beach!'

Hamish's look was steady and intense, carefully perusing Lilly's face as she emerged through the front door.

'Are you up to this, Lilly?'

It was only a minute's walk to the beach. Lilly nodded and managed a smile. She was still floating but she wasn't at all sure that it was the injury and shock of yesterday's events making her feel so strange.

Combination, she thought ruefully. It was a combination of yesterday—and today. Of Hamish being so close. Of Hamish being so concerned.

She'd let herself be drawn down that path before, she thought sadly, walking slowly beside the bouncing barrow. The look in Hamish Campbell's dark eyes was sweet and insidious. How easy to let herself believe that he really did care.

Once at the beach, she was left alone. Hamish set up her air-bed, made sure she had everything she needed and then both males were off to castle construction. Monolith construction, Lilly smiled to herself as she saw the size of their sand castle.

Maybe this was a good idea. Despite Hamish and his unsettling influence, the horrors of yesterday had no reality here. The beach was breathtakingly lovely and Davey's delighted laughter was balm in itself.

She lay watching her son building his castle with his father, drifting in a haze of unreality that contained nothing unpleasant at all. A fairy tale. A fairy tale where the ending was happy ever after.

Halfway through her fairytale, she must have drifted off to sleep.

Heaven knew how long Lilly slept but when she woke Hamish was sitting beside her on the sand, sunlight glinting on a body wet from the surf, and Davey was nowhere to be seen.

Davey. . .

Lilly's eyes flew automatically to the water, searching for Davey, and when she didn't see him she started to rise in panic.

Hamish's hands moved fast to hold her down firmly.

'Davey's up at the house,' he smiled. 'Construction made him hungry so I took him up to Mrs Price and then came back for a proper swim.'

'But. . .' Lilly swallowed. She didn't want to be alone here—with this man. 'But don't you have morning surgery?'

'It's Saturday, in case you haven't noticed, Dr Inger,' Hamish smiled down at her. 'I have surgery between ten and twelve on Saturday mornings and then for another hour at five to cope with sports injuries but, apart from those two sessions and emergencies, Saturday is relatively free. And as it's only eight-thirty now and I have no in-patients at the clinic then I'm free for another hour.'

'And your uncle told me you were overworked,' Lilly muttered.

'Did he?' Hamish raised polite eyebrows. 'I guess the fact that the resort has emptied with the diphtheria scare and every tourist has fled—cutting my workload by half—should have been anticipated by Angus. But it's much easier to believe he lied, isn't it, Lilly?'

Lilly flushed. 'I'm. . .I'm sorry. . .'

'Is that enough?' he asked gently. 'To say sorry when you mistakenly accuse people of lying? When you accused me of lying. . .'

'Isn't Davey positive enough proof that you lied to me?' Lilly muttered, and tried again to rise.

Once again she was pushed back.

'Lilly, stay.'

'I'm not your pet dog,' she snapped and then winced as anger flashed into Hamish's eyes.

'That's not the way you're being treated,' he growled back. 'Not now. Not ever.'

'I'm sorry.' Her voice was flat, devoid of any emotion. 'But. . . Hamish. . .please, I don't want to stay here and talk to you.'

'Why not?'

'We don't have anything to talk about.'

'I think we do,' he said softly. 'I think you deserve some sort of explanation. And I deserve that you listen.'

'There's nothing to explain.'

'Oh, yes, there is,' he said bitterly. He was sitting beside her, staring bleakly out to sea.

His mind was bleak.

Lilly was still lying full-length on her air-bed, watching him with eyes that were cold and filled with pain and he didn't want to see that pain. It reflected his own.

'Lilly, you're the mother of my son,' he said finally, his voice strained and weary. 'Like it or not, we're going to have to see each other while Davey's growing up. Now I know he exists, do you think I'll walk away from him? Even when you leave here I want access, Lilly—regardless of what you think of me. And I'm damned if I'll have you bringing him up with the idea that his father is a heartless, lying bastard.'

'I've never told him that,' Lilly said bleakly.

'So. . . So what have you told him about his father?'

Lilly shrugged. What would Hamish say if he knew the truth? How would he react if he knew what she really had told Davey? The stories she'd told Davey late at night when the little boy was half-asleep and the line between truth and fantasy was blurred to non-existence—that his father was a wonderful man whom she loved with all her heart and one day—one day would come back just like the knights in Davey's book of dragons and princes. . .

She couldn't tell him that. No way.

'I told him his father had to go away,' she said in a voice that was none too steady. 'That's. . .that's all. I guess. . .I guess as he gets older he'll want to know more.'

'And what will you tell him then?' He turned back to face her.

'I. . .' Lilly shrank before the intensity of that look. 'I don't know.'

'Will you tell him you had him because I lied and cheated? That he was a mistake?'

Lilly was silent. There seemed no answer to the bitterness in Hamish's voice.

The bleakness—the bitterness and the anger—was such a contrast to the beauty that was around them! The waves washed in and out again unnoticed. There was only a man and a woman alone on the beach, and the pain of long-remembered heartache.

'I guess. . .I guess I won't tell him that,' she whispered. 'Davey's always known that he was loved and wanted. By his mother at least. When he knows that you're his father I don't. . .I don't want him to know that you didn't want him.'

'I do want him.'

'No.' She rose to sit and face out to sea, hugging her knees under the thin fabric of her dress. The gentle breeze stirred her bright curls round her face, making her achingly aware of the bandage over her ear as the wisps brushed against the gauze.

She felt vulnerable sitting here—and very much alone. More alone even than yesterday facing Wayne Reid.

'Now that you've seen him, you've decided you want him,' she said bitterly. 'Now that your wife is dead, and you've a little replica Hamish Campbell to play with, you've made an easy decision. All joy and no responsibility. . .'

There was a long silence. Hamish was still staring sightlessly out to sea, his eyes blank and solitary.

Man and woman might as well be miles apart.

'I would have wanted him even before my wife was dead,' Hamish said at last. 'If I'd known. . .'

'Don't give me that.' There was anger now, strong and sure, in Lilly's voice. 'Don't give me that line, Hamish Campbell. You must have known I could be pregnant. You knew where to find me. I went straight back to university and you never followed. Not one phone call. Nothing. You lied to me about your inability to father children, your wife comes back, I disappear and you. . .you do nothing. Nothing!'

'Lilly, I have to tell you what happened.'

'I know what happened. I was there, Hamish. Remember?'

'No.' He shook his head and his voice tightened. 'You weren't there. Not when this whole mess started. Not at the start of my marriage. Lilly, I have to tell you now. I should have told you then, but there were things I couldn't bear to talk about.

'There was such joy in finding you and for a while. . . for a while I shoved everything away as if it wasn't important. Being with you—well, it was like coming out from under a huge black cloud and finding that the sun could still shine on my face for a short, sweet while. . .'

Silence. Lilly didn't say a word. She couldn't. She was being forced to listen by something that was stronger than Hamish Campbell's request. Some inner compulsion.

Some need. . .

'I married Lauris when I was a medical student,' Hamish said slowly. 'She was older than I was. I guess. . .I guess you don't know that my father was from a breed known in society as "old money". I'm an only child and. . .well, I'm worth a bit and Lauris knew that. She was working as a television presenter. She was beautiful, talented, vivacious, and the only thing she wanted that she didn't have was to be part of the old money network.

'I was callow, twenty years old, four years younger than Lauris in age but years and years younger in experience and I was a pigeon ripe for the plucking. And as soon as she married me it became perfectly obvious that she'd married me to give her a secure financial base. That was all.'

'All?'

Hamish shrugged. 'There was little else. My parents helped set us up in a house—but there lay the first problem. I wouldn't take any more help from my father than I had to and Lauris had expensive tastes. She wanted to live on my parents' wealth and I wouldn't have a bar of it. Even then.'

Lilly did a fast calculation. Hamish Campbell had graduated eight years before she did. This was all old history—old even when Lilly had met him.

'Oh, the marriage didn't last,' Hamish said shortly, seeing her look and guessing her thoughts. 'Lauris was off even before I finished medical school, moving from one man to another. But I never divorced her.' He shrugged. 'I was immersed in my medicine and my parents hated the idea of me divorcing. It seemed not worth the effort.

'My father, though—well, he was increasingly upset with the idea of no grandchildren. After a few years of seeing Lauris infrequently I decided I should get a divorce. She asked me why—and when I told her I'd like to be free to marry and have children she laughed in my face.

'Said she'd never been on the Pill the whole time we'd been together because she wanted a kid—regardless of what she'd told me then—and nothing had happened. She said she'd had tests and was fine—so it must be me. I was sterile.'

'So?' Despite herself, Lilly was caught up in the story. There was the ring of truth in Hamish's bitter words.

'I was staying down south of Sydney at the time, doing my registrar stint at a provincial hospital,' Hamish went on. 'I decided I should do a sperm count so I sent one off to the local lab—and it came back negative. Nil sperm. It seemed Lauris was right. I was infertile.'

Lilly licked suddenly dry lips. 'But. . .'

'Yeah, "but. . ."' Hamish shrugged. 'Heaven knows how she wangled it but Lauris had friends—contacts—

everywhere. Easy enough to switch samples in a lab, I guess, if you know the right people.'

'But why?'

'I can guess,' Hamish said grimly. 'Now, in retrospect, I can guess. My father was failing even then. Lauris knew a divorce would upset him and I'd only do it for a strong reason. I was immersed in my career. There was no one else. And if Lauris managed to stay married to me until after my father died, then she stood to gain a much, much larger divorce settlement. Huge. Only I was too busy to care very much.

'The sterility thing shocked me—but it just turned me back to my medicine more and more. Lauris could do what she liked. Until. . .until you came along.'

'So. . . So what difference did that make?'

'I guess you know how much,' he said slowly. 'If you remember how we felt. . . What I felt for you then. . .'

Felt. Past tense.

There was balm in the word, though. Balm in Hamish admitting that there had once been something between them. That Davey had been conceived in love. . .

'Only I guess Lauris's network of contacts let her know about you,' Hamish said slowly. 'And you were a threat in the same way as my wanting a child was a threat. So she came back. She talked to you—heaven knows what she said—but when I came back there was only the note.'

'Note?'

Hamish lifted a handful of warm sand and let it trickle idly through his fingers.

'Since I've seen Davey and figured out one of Lauris's lies, I've wondered about the note,' he said softly. 'Did you or did you not write a note when you left?'

'No.'

Hamish nodded. 'I thought not.' He threw the sand down in a harsh, bitter gesture that seemed almost as if he was rejecting the past with the sand. 'Hell!'

'What did. . .what did the note say?'

'The note said that you'd discovered I was married, that I was a lying, cheating bastard and a lot more words to that effect—pure vitriol—and if ever I came near you again you'd take me to the medical board for improper conduct.

'You said it was professionally abhorrent for someone in my position to take advantage of a student. What I'd done was tantamount to rape and you would see me professionally ruined if I ever let anyone know what had happened between us or attempted to come near you.' He shrugged. 'There really wasn't a lot of choice in whether I saw you again.'

'And you believed that?'

He shrugged. 'Why not? There was just enough truth in it to sting. Sure, you were twenty-two but you were still a student and my role was still that of teacher. If you'd wanted to scream professional misconduct, there was no way I could defend myself.' He shrugged again. 'I guess Lauris knew that. She was a very clever woman.'

'But. . .' Lilly chewed her bottom lip. Things were becoming clearer by the minute. No wonder he hadn't followed her. With a threat like that. . .

'I didn't write that note, Hamish.'

'I know that—now.'

Now when it was all too late, his weary voice said. Past history.

'You stayed. . .' There were things she still had to know. 'You stayed with her then for a while, didn't you?' She'd made careful, desperate enquiries in the next few months and Hamish had indeed gone back to living with his wife.

'There were things that didn't add up,' Hamish told her. 'Lauris was still at my flat when I got home. She handed me the note and watched me read it and, then, when I said it didn't make a difference to our marriage—I still wanted a divorce—she burst into tears. For Lauris that was unheard-of.'

'And?'

'Lauris was running scared,' Hamish said dully. 'She'd just been given a life sentence of her own. She had cancer.'

'I. . .I see.'

'It doesn't excuse her,' Hamish went on flatly. 'She probably would have done her damnedest to break us up anyway. But suddenly the beautiful, cool, calculating Lauris was scared stiff. She was alone—and she was my wife. And I had no one else either.'

'So she stayed.'

'It took Lauris eighteen long months to die,' Hamish said grimly. 'And in all that time she never said. . . She never let me know she'd rigged the sperm tests—or written the note herself. There were lies I caught her out in—but not those. It was only when I saw Davey that I realised what she must have done.'

Silence.

Lilly's mind was turning somersaults. The story he was telling her was incredible. . .unbelievable. . .

And yet. . .

She believed him. She thought back to those few short weeks five years ago and remembered Hamish's qualms at their love-making.

'I'm eight years older than you, Lilly,' he'd muttered in a voice thick with passion. 'I shouldn't touch you.'

She'd walked all over his qualms, she remembered, but she knew that he'd had to trust her. She was in a position to make life untenable for him if she'd cried foul.

And for five years he'd believed that was just what she'd done. Cried foul. Threatened him with ruin if he came near her again. . .

What sort of vindictive woman would do that to a man?

A woman dying. A woman wanting to keep her only security at all costs.

Despite the anger—despite the pain of all those barren years—Lilly felt a surge of pity for the dead Lauris. Maybe Lauris's motives in the beginning might have been financial, but she'd needed Hamish for more than money in the end, and who was to say that Lilly's need of him was greater than hers?

There was a kind of peace in the knowledge. Lilly's mind turned over and over and as it did she felt a huge knot of bitterness inside her slowly unravel and fall away.

For five long years Lilly had felt betrayed. She'd felt as if she had put everything she had into loving Hamish Campbell and she had been slapped back like a stupid child asking for more than she deserved.

Now. . .

What now?

Who could say? There was too much bitterness and pain between them to start again. The old love—the passion—was gone. There was no sign of it now in Hamish's attitude to her. But maybe. . . Maybe they could be friends enough to make their shared parenting of Davey a possibility.

Could she stay on the island?

Lilly's mind was still racing. It picked up this possibility, examined it from all sides and rejected it.

No.

Not now.

She might be able to achieve a relationship that wasn't strained at every turn—but she could never relax completely.

She'd been too close to this man. She'd given him her soul—and there was no way she could ask for the return of such a gift. He knew her so intimately that she could never be just a working colleague.

She'd have to go. Maybe not too far—close enough

for Davey to see his father once a week or so—but far enough away. . .

Far enough away for her to keep some semblance of sanity and order for her troubled heart.

She turned from facing the sea to find Hamish watching her with uncertain eyes.

'I'm sorry, Lilly,' he said gently. 'Believe me, I'm sorry.' He held out his hand in an almost formal gesture of friendship. 'You're the mother of my son, Lilly,' he went on, holding her eyes with a look that was steady and true. 'A special, special lady. I betrayed you, but I swear I never meant to. I swear it. Lilly, for Davey's sake—for the next few years we need to be friends. I'm asking for nothing more. I don't want more than friendship, Lilly. I'm making no demands on you—but I do want your friendship.'

'I guess. . .' Lilly whispered. 'I guess you can have that.'

Friendship.

Why did the word sound so darned hollow?

CHAPTER EIGHT

THE media coverage of the diphtheria scare gave the doctors badly needed breathing space.

For the following week there was hardly a tourist on the island. The clinics were quiet and could easily be handled by Hamish. Lilly did most of the house calls, using Dr McVie's wonderful car and often taking Davey with her to explore the island as they puttered from patient to patient.

Lilly needed this time. The shock of her encounter with Wayne Reid was taking its toll, and she found herself tired seemingly for no reason at all.

'The body takes its own measures to heal,' Hamish reassured her when he came into the sunroom on the Saturday afternoon a week from the Reid incident and found Lilly fast asleep on the sofa. She'd opened her eyes with a guilty start as he entered and he'd smiled and told her firmly to stay where she was.

It was a peaceful scene. Davey was doing a jigsaw on the floor beside her, and out in the garden Angus McVie was strolling round the flower-beds with the aid only of his cane.

'And medicines don't always come in a bottle,' Hamish said slowly, his eyes moving from Lilly to her child and then out to Angus in the garden. His gaze stopped at Angus.

'Sometimes,' he smiled, 'medicines come in the form of a young doctor called Lilly and a little boy called Davey.' He shook his head and his smile deepened to a look of contentment. 'You don't know the difference you've made to our Angus, Lilly Inger.'

'Why?' Lilly asked curiously, pushing herself off her cushions to a sitting position and turning to watch

Angus's progress round the garden. She needed to turn her attention from Hamish.

A locum had been booked to start on the island a week from the following Monday. Since he'd told Lilly that, Hamish had been cool and formal with her and the strain was beginning to tell on Lilly. She tended to jump every time she heard a noise behind her—and she had to fight an almost constant desire to burst into tears every time she saw Hamish smile.

It was a reaction from Wayne Reid, she assured herself, but in fact it was more like a reaction to Hamish Campbell's dratted charismatic smile.

Now she again turned her attention determinedly to Angus. The old man was gaining strength every day and there was no doubting his delight in Davey's company.

'Angus is just plain lonely,' Hamish told her, still watching him with affection. 'Angus's wife died ten years ago and he still misses her—aches for her—and their only son died when he wasn't much more than Davey's age.'

'He has you.' This was the first time that Hamish's formal tone had slipped and Lilly was prepared to make the most of it.

'And I have Angus,' Hamish agreed. 'Angus has always been more like a father to me than my own father. My dad spent his life worrying about money. Angus spends his worrying about people—and I know which I'd prefer.'

'Hamish, why did you give up surgery and come here?' Lilly asked curiously—still careful not to look at him. 'Did Angus want you to come into partnership with him?'

Hamish shook his head. 'Just as Lauris died, Angus had his first coronary,' he told her. 'It was a minor one but a warning all the same. He had to rest. The problem was that Angus has been on this island for forty years and he couldn't bear to leave. At that time the resort was only in its infancy and there wasn't a large enough population to support two doctors. No stranger would accept a partnership with Angus, knowing that when Angus recovered every islander would prefer to use him.

'So Angus was faced with leaving—or accepting my offer to come and work with him. Because we share a house and housekeeper I could make do on a lesser income, and gradually I've become accepted by the islanders to the extent that I'm just as much in demand as Angus—even before he had the second coronary.'

'But your career... Your surgery...'

'It's funny how little I miss the career ladder,' Hamish told her reflectively. 'I sure as hell don't miss it enough to quit the island and force Angus to leave here.'

'And when he dies?' Lilly looked out at Angus's frail figure and knew that his death was a possibility at any time.

'I'll cross that bridge when I come to it—but I'm hoping we'll have him round for a while longer yet.' Hamish had crossed to the window, gazing out through the garden to the sea beyond. It seemed as if he was almost talking to himself.

'Sure, Angus's health has gone backwards over the last few weeks but he's been under strain I couldn't prevent. With the resort growing to its current size, we really do need two doctors. I've done the best I could but if a call came while I was out on another Angus went out, regardless of how often I ordered him not to. He had a few really late nights before his second attack—and then there was the strain of knowing you were coming...'

'Was he really afraid I'd take my anger out on him?' Lilly asked and Hamish smiled.

'No. But he was afraid I'd be angry. Or upset. he doesn't like people to be unhappy, my uncle Angus.'

Davey looked up from his puzzle. 'Who's unhappy?' he queried. 'I'm not.' His small brow clouded. 'But I might be in a week when I have to leave,' he said sadly.

'I might be in a week, too,' Hamish confessed, smiling down at his son. He stooped to lift Davey and swing him up into his arms. 'You're getting to be habit-forming, young Davey.' He stood, holding Davey close, their brilliant red hair merging, and he looked back down at Lilly.

'I do have one suggestion, though. I've been thinking over the past few days. Wondering whether we could come to some sort of arrangement. I understand. . .' he hesitated '. . .I understand you don't wish to stay here in this house, and I guess I agree with you. There's talk round the island already—with Davey looking like he does.

'But maybe if we found you both another cottage to live in. . . Somewhere close so you could drop Davey off here to stay with Mrs Price and Angus when you were called out. . .'

Stay living on the island? Stay with Hamish—and yet not?

Lilly closed her eyes.

At first glance the idea had instant appeal. This place—this island—was wonderful. It felt like home.

It felt like home because Hamish was here, she knew. Hamish was her heart and her home. He'd been that since the moment she'd met him—and yet here he was looking at her like she was some dear memory. He regarded her as part of his past that was sweetly remembered but there was no hint that past fires could be rekindled.

He'd had a wife once. A wife who seemed to have drained him of everything. There was no indication that Hamish was in the market for another woman.

And how would she feel, spending the rest of her years being treated as just that—a memory Hamish Campbell was fond of? A friend. The mother of his son. Someone he'd come to 'an arrangement' with.

She was going to have to face it anyway, she told herself bitterly, but better to spend her time away from here so that every time she looked round—every time she walked into a room and found him or saw him over a breakfast table—she didn't feel her heart wrench.

'I will leave,' she said gently. 'Hamish, I must. . .'

'Because of me?'

'Yes.' There was no other answer to give.

'Do you hate me so much, then?'

'I don't hate you,' she said carefully. Hate? How far from the truth could that be? 'But. . . Hamish, I don't want to live near you.'

'Lilly, I need to be near Davey,' he said flatly and Lilly nodded. It was Davey this man was interested in now. She was only the mother of his son. It was an unbearable thought. . .

'I won't go so far you can't see him,' she answered, her voice somehow flat and emotionless. 'Not. . .not if you wish to form a relationship with him. But if I work in Cairns—or even Townsville—then you'll be able to see him often.'

'Not often enough.'

'I can't. . .I can't do any better than that,' Lilly whispered. 'I'm sorry, Hamish. . .'

He closed his eyes. 'I'm sorry too,' he told her bleakly. 'You don't know how sorry.' Then he shrugged. 'But if you won't bend, then this locum has to come. I must have someone or I'm risking Angus working again.'

End of argument. She would be more satisfactory because Angus liked Davey and Hamish also wanted Davey, but if she was going to be stubborn. . .

Lilly was going to be stubborn. There was nothing else for Lilly to be.

The phone went at that moment and Lilly saw Hamish disappear to answer it with a sense of relief. She helped Davey with three pieces of jigsaw and then looked up again as Hamish re-entered the room.

'I've a house call up on Lightning Ridge,' Hamish

said from the doorway. 'Lilly—Dr Inger—I wonder if you'd like to come.'

Lilly examined Hamish's face with care. He'd snapped back into professional mode when the phone rang and now his face was bland, carefully wiped free of any expression.

'Why?' she said flatly.

The bland expression stayed. 'There's no need to sound so suspicious, Dr Inger. I just thought— Lightning Ridge is a great part of the island with views almost to Hawaii, and you haven't been up there before.'

She checked his eyes again. 'Why, Hamish Campbell?'

The blandness broke and Hamish's eyes creased into involuntary laughter. 'You have a nasty, suspicious mind. . .'

'I know you,' she smiled and then grimaced inwardly. She did know Hamish Campbell all too well. Every expression this man possessed, she knew by heart.

'It's just—my patient might appreciate a lady doctor. . .'

'It's hysterics,' Lilly said suspiciously, carefully watching his face. 'You don't look worried enough to need me for plain medical reasons. My guess is that you have a teenage girl suffering from hysterics. Either that or you have a lady who has a "miscarriage" once a month and insists on an internal examination at home. Which is it, Dr Campbell?'

His smile deepened. 'You're an astute woman, Lilly Inger.'

'Flattery will get you nowhere.'

'How about I confess it's teenage hysteria and say please really, really nicely?'

Lilly gave in. She spread her hands in a gesture of defeat, smiled back and rose to her feet. 'Well. . . Seeing you confessed. Tell me where to go, Dr Campbell, and I'll do it for you.'

'If Davey's happy here then maybe we should go together,' Hamish told her. His grin slipped. 'Lilly, Mrs Burn who rang is a sensible farmer's wife, and she says Claire—her sixteen-year-old—"is off the planet". For a lady not prone to exaggeration, things sound pretty much out of control. So while I might not need you medically. . .'

Lilly nodded. Pure, over-the-top hysteria in teenagers was often the result of family argument, and doctors called to help often found more than one patient—Mum in tears, Dad threatening to shoot a boyfriend if he ever showed his face—and all sorts of situations, none of which were pleasant.

'I'll come,' Lilly sighed. 'Can you finish the jigsaw on your own, Davey?'

'Course I can.' Hamish had placed Davey back in front of the jigsaw when the phone went and now the little boy didn't even look up. 'You only do the easy bits anyway, Mum. If it's really hard then Uncle Angus will help.'

Uncle Angus. . .

The name had come from nowhere. Angus had been as surprised as any of them when Davey had changed to that form of addressing him—but there was no doubting that both the old man and the little boy welcomed their relationship with joy.

How soon would it be before Davey figured out the other connection?

How soon before Davey started calling Hamish 'Daddy'?

Lilly winced. This all hurt so much. It was like a constant, physical ache—a toothache that refused to go away but the pain wasn't just in a sore tooth. It was in every last part of her.

She had to get away from here.

'Bring your swimming gear,' Hamish was telling her, his eyes vaguely troubled as he watched her. It was as if he sensed her pain—but that he had troubles of his own and there was nothing he could do about hers.

There was nothing anyone could do about Lilly's pain. Hamish Campbell might be a good and intuitive doctor but there was no known cure for what was troubling Lilly.

'Swimming gear?' she asked doubtfully.

'There's a waterfall up on the ridge,' Hamish told her. 'It's on the Burns' land and we're welcome to swim there. It truly is spectacular, Lilly—and if you're dead set on leaving at the end of the week—'

'Why wouldn't I be?' Lilly asked with more bitterness than she'd intended—and Hamish nodded.

'I'm not questioning your intentions,' Hamish said gently. 'It's just that if you're leaving in a week then maybe you should see as much of the island as you can.'

See as much of the island. . .

See as much of Hamish Campbell. . .

They took Angus's car.

'I love it,' Hamish told her as they puttered along the ocean road and the wind blew Lilly's hair out in a golden stream behind her. 'I use it whenever I can.' He smiled across at the girl beside him. 'And don't say you didn't notice the look in Angus's eyes as he saw us drive off in it. This car is one of his chief delights and he loves us using it.'

'And you love pleasing him,' Lilly added softly.

Hamish's attitude to his elderly uncle was a side of the man she hadn't seen before, and it strengthened the way she felt about him. Five years ago Lilly Inger had judged Hamish Campbell to be one of the most caring, compassionate men she'd ever met—and her initial judgement had been right. It was being proved over and over.

He was a father for Davey to be proud of.

Lilly faced the road ahead, setting her lips in a tight line and refusing absolutely to allow the sudden welling

of moisture behind her eyes to go any further. Crazy. . .
What she still felt was crazy. . .

She tried hard to concentrate on the scenery. Hamish
was right. This really was a spectacular part of the
island—a high ridge along the island's mountains, with
the sea stretched out on all sides of them. In the distance,
to the west, she could see the Australian mainland—
but to the east there was nothing but miles and miles
of ocean, stretching for ever.

'I feel like I'm on top of the world here—literally,'
Hamish told her and Lilly flushed. He sensed her
thoughts. This man knew her well.

He didn't sense everything.

High on this ridge she might really be on top of
the world but in her heart—in her heart she was
anything but.

This was crazy. How she was feeling was just stupid,
stupid emotion. Hamish had told her flatly that he
wanted no more relationships—ever. So why on earth
couldn't she keep her emotions under control?

Impossible task. . .

Finally, to Lilly's relief, they turned down the track
to the Burns' house. An empty four-gallon drum stuck
on a post to serve as mailbox proclaimed it as the Burns'
property, but the drum was set back off the road and if
Hamish hadn't come Lilly doubted whether she would
have found the place.

The farm was like no farm Lilly had ever known.
Hamish steered the little car down a rutted, dirt track.
Vast gums towered overhead and thick undergrowth
brushed the sides of Angus's precious car, and the
further they went the deeper grew Lilly's curiosity.

'What sort of farm is this, for heaven's sake?'

'The Burn family farms flowers,' Hamish told her.
'They sell proteas, banksias and lots of traditional
Australian wild flowers to the florists on the mainland,
and they also export to Japan. They own about five
hundred acres but only about thirty acres are under

flowers. The rest they leave as old forest—and every parrot and cockatoo on the island loves them for it.'

They surely did. The bird noise was almost deafening, and in the cleared slit made for the track there were constant flashes of colourful native birds.

'It's beautiful,' Lilly sighed softly. 'Just beautiful.'

Hamish glanced across at her. 'There's no need to sound so sad,' he said gently. 'You can stay on the island if you want.'

Lilly bit her lip and shook her head.

'I don't. . .I don't want.'

She didn't know what she wanted.

The Burns were waiting for them in force as they rounded the next bend.

On the veranda of the farm cottage a middle-aged farmer, his wife and two children aged about ten and twelve were waiting for them. They all looked equally worried and as Hamish parked Angus's car the farmer strode down to grasp Hamish by the hand and draw him to the house.

'Thank God you're here, Doc,' the farmer said gratefully. 'We're that worried. The kid's off the air.'

Hamish stopped dead a few feet from the car, refusing to be drawn further. Lilly collected the medical bag and joined him, also resisting the farmer's efforts to haul them quickly into the house. To be drawn into the fray without a prior briefing was asking for trouble.

'Tell me what the trouble is first,' Hamish ordered. He introduced Lilly and then stood firm until an explanation was forthcoming.

It took some time.

Father and mother looked at each other and then from Hamish to Lilly—and then back to each other.

'We. . .we don't know,' the farmer admitted at last. The big farmer's face creased in anguish. 'Heck, Doc. . . All we know is that Claire screams every time we come near.'

'Has there been some argument?' Hamish asked gently, and looked round at the family members. Even the children seemed to be scared.

That just about summed up the family's attitude, Lilly thought slowly. This family weren't in the midst of some family brawl. They were all just plain frightened. There were things going on that they didn't understand.

'It's not a fight. . .' It was Mrs Burn speaking. She was much smaller than her husband, pretty with a dumpy, built-for-comfort figure and attractive blue eyes—but her fear was showing through as clear as day. 'There should have been a fight—or at least a telling-off but—'

'Claire's been out all night,' her husband interrupted roughly. 'The kid went to her friend's sixteenth birthday last night—Debbie Fraser's—and her boyfriend said he'd drive her home. I didn't like the idea, but Steven promised to have her home by midnight and she nagged so much. . .

'Anyway, she didn't come home—she rang at midnight and said Steven's car had broken down so she was staying at Debbie's. I spoke to Debbie's mum and she said it was fine but I was worried. To be honest— well, Debbie's mum's not as fussy as we are but Claire was adamant she'd be fine and when I said I'd come and get her she burst into tears and said I didn't trust her.'

He sighed heavily and dug his hands deep into his pockets. 'I shouldn't have. . .'

'Her boyfriend's Steven Carter, isn't he?' Hamish queried.

'Yes.'

'And this morning?' Hamish prompted.

'This morning Steven's car was miraculously better and he brought her home,' the farmer said. 'He drove her here and practically threw her out of the car and couldn't get out of the place fast enough. Said he had to start work at nine across at the resort—he works as a gardener there. And we started asking Claire questions and she just sort of withdrew—and she's been getting stranger and stranger all day.'

The farmer's hands came out of his pockets in the gesture of a man who didn't know where to put them.

'We thought it was because she was scared of getting into trouble. But it's more than that. We can't talk to her. She acts like she's expecting to be tortured and she knows we don't punish our kids like that. I mean. . . Well, she might expect to be grounded or something but not hit. Never hit.' The farmer spread his hands. 'She scares us, and that's the truth, Doc.'

'She's not rational,' Mrs Burn whispered. 'She acts like she doesn't even know who we are. Even if something dreadful happened. . .' She gulped. 'Even if. . . Well, she'd know. Our Claire would know we'd always stand by her. But she just keeps screaming.'

'OK.' Hamish nodded abruptly to Lilly, their eyes meeting in a moment of shared dismay. They could both sense what they'd be facing now. 'Let's see her.'

Their shared instinct was right.

This was no ordinary bout of teenage hysteria. Claire Burn was well beyond that.

Claire was in her bedroom, crouched at the head of her bed in a position that was as near to foetal as she could make it. The teenager looked out at her family with wide, terrified eyes and as Lilly and Hamish stood in the doorway she shrank back as if she wanted to melt into the wall.

Her long, black hair was dishevelled, her clothes looked as though they'd been slept in and her face was swollen with tears and streaked with smudged mascara.

Hamish took one step towards her and she started to scream.

This wasn't the normal scream of hysteria.

Hysterical screaming was almost a message of 'come one step closer and I'll scream so loud I'll burst your eardrums'. This wasn't like that. Claire's scream was of pure, unmitigated horror. Her hands went up to shield her face, as if Hamish were walking toward her with an unsheathed knife.

Hamish stopped dead.

'Claire, it's the doctor. . .' Mrs Burn was walking in behind Hamish but her protest was futile. Claire's terror didn't abate one whit. She seemed just as terrified of her mother as she was of Hamish.

Lilly put a hand on the woman's arm and pulled her gently out of the room.

'Leave her be, Mrs Burn,' she said softly. 'It's useless talking. She can't hear you when she's like that.'

Lilly drew all the family out, leaving Hamish inside. She'd return to him in a moment. . .but first. . .

She closed the bedroom door, shutting Hamish in with Claire's terror.

'Mrs Burn, has Claire ever tried drugs that you know of?' she asked gently.

'Drugs. . .?' It was the farmer who spoke. Henry Burn whistled soundlessly and his hands clenched and unclenched. 'You mean. . . You mean like heroin and marihuana and stuff. . .?'

'Yes.' There was no point in wrapping this up nicely.

'She wouldn't. . .' Mrs Burn breathed. She looked doubtfully up to her husband. 'Claire wouldn't be so stupid. . . Would she?'

'She might if that bloody boyfriend of hers told her to,' the farmer spat, his face white and appalled as he realised what Lilly was suggesting. He grimaced down at Lilly and then winced as the screaming from inside the bedroom became ear-splitting. 'Or if she thought it'd impress him. She's that pleased he asked her out and she and her mum had a fight because she reckoned her dress made her look too young. But if he made her. . .'

'You think it's possible there were drugs at the party she went to?'

'I wouldn't have let her go if I'd thought that,' Mrs

Burn gasped, wiping frightened tears away with her apron. 'Oh, dear heaven. . .' She clutched Lilly's arm. 'Do you think that's what this is? An overdose or something?'

'It's what it looks like,' Lilly told them. 'My guess is she's taken LSD or something similar and is hallucinating. Sometimes a drug like LSD has this effect on people who haven't used it before. With your permission, we'll give her a sedative and she should slowly settle over the next few hours.'

'But. . . But she'll be OK?'

'I've seen this happen before,' Lilly told them. 'It does settle. But we do need your permission for the diazepam.'

'Our permission. . . You need. . .' The farmer gazed down at Lilly in horror. 'Oh, yeah. . .' he whispered. 'Of course you have our permission.' He wrung his hands as Lilly turned to re-enter the bedroom. 'If I get my hands on that bloody Steven I'll kill him. . .'

Hamish was not coping on his own. He wasn't trying to. He'd stopped a few feet from the bed and was attempting to talk soothingly to Claire but she would have none of it. She was trembling like a frightened rabbit before a pack of terriers and Lilly's heart went out to her.

Stupid kids. They took these things without the least idea how their bodies would react—and sometimes their bodies just couldn't take it.

As least it wasn't an overdose of heroin. If it had been. . . If it had been, Claire could well have already been dead.

'I have permission for a sedative,' she told Hamish softly, her eyes on Claire, and Hamish nodded.

'OK. Can you prepare it?'

'You think it's LSD?' Lilly asked, watching Claire's huge, dilated eyes.

'It's the obvious diagnosis,' Hamish said grimly. 'If

she was at a party with Debbie Fraser. . . Debbie's mum
is as silly as a tin of worms, and she'll have exerted no
control.'

'But. . .' Lilly frowned. 'A sixteenth birthday
party. . . I can understand alcohol abuse, but where
would they get drugs?'

'Someone's pushing them on the island at the
moment,' Hamish growled. 'I've had a few instances
like this over the last few months—and the local police
reckon there's a pusher. They've been watching Wayne
Reid—but now he's in gaol—'

'He could have supplied this before he was arrested
last week,' Lilly told him. She was bending over the
medical bag, filling a syringe with valium, and watching
Hamish edge closer to the bed as she did.

'He might have,' Hamish said gravely. 'He's been
on the island long enough. I'd like to think we had the
problem licked—but somehow I doubt it. I can't see
Steven making Claire take drugs. All the same, I'd like
to have a good long talk with Claire's Steven.'

Claire had subsided slightly. Hamish looked across
at Lilly and raised his eyebrows in silent query. Lilly
nodded. The syringe was ready.

'OK, Claire. . .'

There was no response. Her terror was palpable. Lilly
watched Hamish brace himself.

Ideally for this procedure there should have been a
couple of hospital orderlies. Maybe they could have
asked Claire's parents to assist, but their distress might
well have made them more of a hindrance than a help.
Hopefully, Claire was small enough for Hamish to cope
with on his own.

Hamish moved. There was nothing Lilly could do.
With the syringe in her hand, she had to stay well clear
of flailing arms and legs. She stood back, waiting. . .

She didn't have to wait long. Where Hamish had
learned to immobilise someone Lilly didn't know, but
she could only shake her head in disbelief. In one deft

movement—almost before the hysterical girl could realise what was happening—Hamish had caught her, locked her arms, twisted her over and was pressing her gently but firmly face-down into the soft bedcovers.

'Now!'

Lilly moved with equal speed and the syringe of valium was emptied speedily into the top of Claire's thigh.

Claire was gasping and choking—sobbing with mingled fright and rage—but Hamish didn't release her. He held the girl tight and Lilly sat down at the head of the bed beside her. If they released her now she might well try to fight them off or escape—and heaven knew what damage she could do to herself.

'Hush, Claire,' Lilly said gently, over and over again, and softly stroked the girl's tangled hair. 'Hush. The medicine will work in a moment and you'll be fine. Hush. . .'

It took ten minutes before the fight went out of her.

They felt rather than saw the sedative take effect. The terror holding the girl rigid suddenly released its hold. Claire's slight body slackened in Hamish's grip. The sobbing faded to rasping breathing and the girl slumped into exhausted sleep.

Hamish held her for a few moments longer and then he nodded to Lilly.

'OK. I'll go and talk to her parents.'

'I'll get her out of her clothes,' Lilly said, still stroking the child's head. 'If she wakes up in her nightie in her own bed she's much less likely to go off the air again.'

Hamish nodded and smiled wearily at her, knowing what else Lilly had to do now and relieved that she was there to do it for him.

'Thanks, Lilly. You're a blessing.' His smile faded. 'If we could just find the bastard that's doing this to our kids. . .'

*   *   *

They left half an hour later.

Claire was still soundly sleeping.

'She may well sleep till morning,' Hamish told the parents. 'It's what she needs. She mustn't be left alone, though. Can you watch her and ring me again the moment you're worried?'

'We'll watch her like a hawk,' Mrs Burn said grimly. She was sitting next to her daughter's bed, her hand gripping her daughter's as if she would never release it. She looked up at Lilly. 'You're sure. . .? You're sure. . .? If they gave her drugs. . . You're sure. . .?'

'She hasn't been interfered with,' Lilly said definitely. It had been her biggest fear, too. Often young girls were offered drugs to make them easy targets, but this hadn't been the case for Claire. 'I've checked thoroughly, Mrs Burn, and I'm absolutely sure.'

The farmer gaped from one to the other and what they were talking about sank home with a sickening thud. 'If that lout touched her. . .'

'I'll speak to Steven myself and find out exactly what's happened,' Hamish told the angry farmer. He laid a hand on his shoulder. 'But for now. . . For now, accept the fact that Steven brought her home, he hasn't taken advantage of her drugged state and there seems no long-term damage done. Let's not blame the boy yet until we know all the facts.'

'So you get to interview the boyfriend?' Lilly queried, as they finally left the sleeping Claire to her worried parents.

'Mmm.' Hamish seemed deep in thought as he steered back down the farm track. 'I know Steven Carter, though, and it's not making sense. He's not a bad kid. He's not terribly intelligent—he dropped out of school last year to take a gardening job and he's likely to be content with being a gardener's lad for life—but there's no harm in him. His mum's lovely. I can't see him pushing drugs.' He shook his head.

'There's no street cunning in Steven. He'd never make it as a drug dealer.'

'Maybe he just bought the drug, persuaded Claire to take it and then got scared,' Lilly suggested and Hamish shook his head.

'I can't see it.' He grimaced. 'I saw Steven when I was over at the resort last week and he told me he'd finally persuaded Claire's parents to let her come out with him. Pleased as Punch, he was—and proud.

'I must admit when I heard they were going out together I thought it could well last. Claire's a bit silly but she's young and she's basically a good kid, too, and it wouldn't have surprised me to find Steven eventually working for her old man and making it a family affair.' He glanced at his watch. 'Steven plays cricket on Saturday afternoon. I'll catch him afterwards.' He glanced across at Lilly.

'Which means we still have time to check out this waterfall. OK?'

'I don't. . . Shouldn't we be getting back?' Lilly asked, a trifle breathlessly.

'I'd rather not.' Hamish motioned to the mobile phone on the seat beside him. 'It's a half-hour drive from home to here—and I wouldn't mind staying in range for an hour or so. If Claire's going to get worse the drug reaction will break through the diazepam and if we're at the waterfall we can get back within five minutes.'

There was no argument for logic like that. Lilly had nothing to fight with.

Why did she want to fight?

She didn't want to fight at all, she thought wearily. It was just that she didn't want to spend one more moment with Hamish Campbell than she absolutely had to.

This man had the power to tear her apart.

CHAPTER NINE

HAMISH produced his waterfall as a magician produced a rabbit from a hat.

He drove the short distance down into a valley to the falls, the sound of rushing water growing louder as they descended. A final twist in the road brought the falls into full view. Hamish brought the car to a halt and then turned to watch Lilly's expression.

Lilly's face was everything Hamish could have wished.

She would have been blind to be impervious to this beauty. Lilly gazed slowly around, awestruck by the majesty of the cascading water and the waterfall's surrounds.

This place seemed untouched by mankind. The forests growing round the falls consisted of massive eucalypts reaching for the sky, and a soft understorey of matted leaves, rotting logs—and thousands and thousands of tiny, fragile native orchids.

The orchids were the size of fingernails, each one creamy white with a soft pink to purple throat. Together they looked like a delicate, silken carpet—a carpet spun for kings.

Lilly climbed cautiously from the car—the orchids were so close she was scared almost to put her feet down—and stared round in wonder.

'I never knew a place as beautiful as this existed,' she breathed.

Her words were lost in the sounds of cascading water. The stream poured its load down over rocks in a glorious, tumbling mass that made Lilly reach back into the car for her swimming gear without a second thought.

The rock pool at the base of the falls was crystal clear and calling a translucent invitation.

Lilly couldn't resist such a summons. The valley was still and hot and the water looked wonderful.

She looked doubtfully across at Hamish but he was smiling and signalling her to go behind a pile of fallen logs and change.

'Dressing-rooms, my lady,' he called over the sound of the water and Lilly nodded and turned away. Hamish still had the power to make her blush for no reason at all—but, despite how Hamish Campbell made her feel, she was going to savour this swim.

Five minutes later Lilly emerged from her strange dressing-room, carefully picking her way over the orchids to the water's edge. She wasn't going to squash an orchid if she could help it!

Hamish was nowhere to be seen.

She looked dubiously round, expecting him to emerge as she had from behind some of the fallen timber, but he didn't show.

No Hamish.

So much the better.

If he'd gone for a walk by himself then she could have a few moments to savour this magic place without self-consciousness.

For one long moment Lilly stood still on the side of the pool at the base of the falls, gazing down into its crystal depths with increasing delight. The water was deep. She could see a few flashes of silver—minnows darting among the rocks ten or maybe twelve feet down. More maybe. Certainly deep enough to dive. She took a deep breath and then arrowed her body down, darting like the fish down into the clear depths.

The water was freezing.

Lilly emerged to break the surface spluttering and laughing. She'd expected the warmth of the subtropical ocean but this water was from the heights of the mountains, crisp and cold. Its iciness made her gasp.

It was still beautiful.

Her body gradually adjusted to the cold. Lilly rolled over onto her back and floated, looking upward at the trees. The leaves of the huge, overhanging gums dappled sunlight over her face, and peace descended like a mist. Only the shrill sounds of the native birds rose over the noise of the water.

But where was Hamish?

Increasingly, not knowing where the man was disturbed her calm.

Would he have gone for a walk in the bush without telling her? Lilly looked out over the banks of the pool and there was the car parked nearby in its oasis of orchids—and nothing else.

No one.

Maybe Hamish just wanted to be alone. Like her.

Liar. She didn't want to be alone. She'd had enough of being alone to last a lifetime.

Well, like it or not, she was alone now and she was just going to have to make the most of it. She didn't know where Hamish was but he wasn't a child. She shouldn't worry.

She shouldn't.

Ha! Lilly proceeded straight to worry in one fast step. What if he'd tripped while she was changing? What if he'd struck his head and fallen into the water?

Oh, for heaven's sake. . . If he'd fallen in she'd see his body in this clear water, and she'd seen enough of his water skills at the beach to know the man swam like a fish.

She was being ridiculous. What Hamish was doing was his business. She was here to enjoy herself, so she might as well get right on and do just that.

So. . . So enjoy yourself, Lilly Inger, she told herself firmly. Lilly took a deep breath, looked across at the cascading waterfall, put her head down and swam right into the tumbling force of water.

The plummeting water pushed her down as she dived

into the maelstrom. It flung her over and over, and tossed her back out into the calm pool like a limp rag doll.

The sensation was indescribable. Wonderful! If she could lift this magic combination of power and beauty and transfer it to an aquatic fun park, she could make a fortune ten times over selling tickets.

Lilly took a few gasping breaths, checked the falls for the point where the flow seemed least and tried again. It'd be great to reach the back of the falls. If she could somehow get behind that cascade. . . It looked like there was some sort of ledge behind. Maybe a cave. . .

Another breath. She dived down and tried again.

Same thing.

The water treated her like it'd treat an inert object, bouncing her out when she didn't want to be bounced.

It was starting to be a real challenge. One more try, Lilly. Once more.

She glared at the waterfall, daring it to defy her one more time, grinned a bit at her own silliness and tried again. She dived deep, hard into the falls, the water pounded down, she started sinking. . .

And something gripped and held.

For one split second she reacted with horror. To be held in that force of water. . .

But the force gripping her was a human hand. She was being pulled up backward out of the force of the massive sheet of water behind the cascade to the ledge beyond.

Hamish. . .

Hamish was drawing her up to the ledge behind the falls to the entrance to a cave. A cave like no cave Lilly had ever seen.

Her body was limp with shock. She let herself be drawn up, powerless either to resist or aid. Finally, as her body lifted clear of the water, she gathered enough of her wits to help Hamish pull her over onto the ledge.

To sit beside Hamish.

'I thought you were never coming,' Hamish laughed at her, his streaming wet body skin to skin against hers on the ledge. The ledge behind the water was only just wide enough for the two of them to sit side by side, with a tiny cave recessed into the rocks behind them. 'I had tea and toast all made and ready,' he complained. 'But it went cold while I waited.'

'Oh, yeah?' Lilly choked. 'So where is it now?'

'I ate it,' he grinned. 'What else? And I've packed the silver tea service back into the sideboard at the back of the cave for next time.'

Next time. . .

Somehow Lilly managed to chuckle. She sat on her ledge and looked out through the translucent sheet of water hiding her from the outside world. This place was surreal. A paradise cut off from reality. And she was here—in her paradise. With the man she loved.

With a man who didn't love her.

Her forced laughter died.

Hamish Campbell treated her with affection but nothing else. He was laughing with her now as he'd laugh with Davey. Only with Davey there was a long-term relationship to be forged. With Lilly there was nothing.

'What's wrong, Lilly?' Hamish asked gently. Some freak of nature in this eerie place made the sound of the water echo outward. The thunder outside was now a muted sigh, and every word they uttered in the small chamber echoed around and behind them. It was a weirdly intimate setting.

'Nothing's wrong.' Lilly pushed her streaming curls from her face and tried to look cheerful. 'What could be wrong? This. . .this place is beautiful.'

'But you'll still leave?'

'The island. . .?' Lilly swallowed. 'I. . . Yes. I'll still leave the island.'

'Why?'

'I don't. . . I. . . Hamish, I must.'

'You can't bear to be near me.'

She nodded. There was no denying it. 'That's right, Hamish,' she whispered. 'I don't. . .I don't want to be near you any more.'

He sat silent for a long moment, like Lilly staring out through the pane of moving water. 'Lilly, I know I was a bastard. . .' he said slowly.

'It's not. . .'

'Not what?'

Lilly closed her eyes. 'Hamish, you've told me what happened all those years ago. I believe you. It's not. . . It's not dislike of you that's driving me away. It's just. . . Hamish, what was between us. . .I can't just put it aside as if it never happened and get on with my life. Not with you here reminding me.'

'And you don't want to be reminded.'

What on earth did he expect her to say to that? There was only one answer to give really. Only one word.

'No.' Lilly flinched. A shiver ran through her still-wet body. The ledge they were sitting on was tiny—room really only for one yet they were pressed together side by side. Hamish felt her shiver—and drew slightly away.

It was as if he wasn't here to give comfort. He was here to get at some unpalatable truth.

There were plenty of better places to speak unpalatable truths, Lilly thought bitterly, anger staring to grow. What sort of game did this man think he was playing?

'I think. . .I think it's time we went. . .' she started.

'Back to the house, you mean?' Hamish asked her. 'You want to go back to your wall of silence.'

'What. . .what do you mean?'

'You've hardly talked to me all week, Lilly. Yet when I knew you. . .' He shrugged. 'You were. . .you were happy when I first knew you. You bubbled and chattered like a butcher's magpie. And it's gone.'

'Five years ago I was happy,' Lilly said softly. 'Five

years is a long time, Hamish. I'm a different woman.'

'Are you?'

'Yes.' It was said flatly, unemotionally—as if she really meant it. Only her body betrayed her with its stupid trembling and Lilly willed herself to stop it. To stay rigid and still—and emotionless—was the only way she could cope.

'Angus really wants you to stay here,' Hamish said softly.

Angus wants you. . .

Oh, great. Angus wanted her to stay. Davey wanted her to stay. And Hamish?

Hamish didn't want her to stay enough.

'I can't.'

'Lilly, I have another suggestion.'

Lilly's body stilled of its own accord. There was something in Hamish's voice that was a warning. Usually calm, deep and resonant, his voice was suddenly unsure.

'Y-yes?'

Hamish was still not looking at her. He was watching the sheet of water in front of him. Now he put out a hand to catch its flow and the sheet diverted, sending a shower of water back over his almost naked body.

He seemed almost to welcome its presence. The spray of water stopped the weird intimacy. It cut him off from Lilly.

'I'd like you to marry me.'

Silence.

'What. . .what did you say?' Lilly managed at last, her voice barely more than a whisper.

Still Hamish didn't look at her. All his attention was on the water. His body was still touching hers but it was rigid and. . .

And repelling.

'I know I don't have any rights where you're concerned,' Hamish told her flatly. 'I lost those five years ago. I should have guessed you might be pregnant—or

at least found out where you were. I didn't. So I lost. . .I
lost contact with you. And I lost my son.'

My son.

The word rang out between them. My son. So Davey
was what this was all about.

'Hamish, no. . .'

'Lilly, think about it,' Hamish demanded. He turned
to her and his hands came up to grasp her shoulders.
She shrank back from his touch but his hands stayed.
'I'm asking you to at least consider. . .'

Consider marrying Hamish? Lilly stared up at the
man holding her, her heart pounding so hard she could
almost hear it. Marry Hamish? Lilly had done little else
but consider that option for five long years.

'Wh-why?' she whispered. Somehow she had to
make sense of what was happening. Somehow.

'It makes sense.' His words echoed her thought.
Hamish was looking directly at her now, his dark eyes
searching hers—trying to read what was in her mind.

'I've thought it out and it could work. You won't
stay on the island with Davey and I can understand that.
Half the island has guessed he's my son now, and your
position is untenable. Angus pointed it out to me and
he's right. The islanders know my wife died three years
ago and they've guessed Davey is my son. If you stay
here you'll be branded my ex-mistress for life.'

'So. . . So you'll change my title. From previous mis-
tress to current wife.' Lilly's words were a tremulous
whisper.

'If you think. . .' Still the hands held her and still his
eyes searched. 'Lilly, if you think you could bear it.'
His grip tightened. 'I know. . .I hurt you so badly when
you were just a kid. God knows I never meant to, and
I'm paying for it now. I paid for it then. But I can make
it up to you now, Lilly. I can give you security. I can
give Davey a father—share your responsibilities and
make sure you're financially secure. I'll look after you,
Lilly. I swear.'

'Give me a home in my old age. . .' Lilly choked.

'Give you companionship,' Hamish said softly. 'We can be friends, Lilly. I know it. I can't expect any more of our marriage than that, but you'll have my friendship. And if that's what you want then it'll stop at that. God knows, I married for passion once—and look where that got me.'

'So you wouldn't be marrying for. . .for passion?'

'We had passion between us once,' Hamish said gently. 'Maybe we could rekindle it—if that's what you want. But I swear I'll exert no pressure on you, Lilly.' He let his hands fall from her shoulders to her bare arms, and his eyes searched her face. 'Lilly, it could be a good life. Angus already loves you and he loves Davey. Mrs Price thinks you're the best thing since sliced bread. And me. . .' He smiled. 'I'd have a wife I'd be proud of.'

Neat solution. Lilly stared back at Hamish, her eyes clouded with doubts. Neat solution.

Why did it sound so. . .?

So desolate?

There was only one answer to this crazy proposition. One answer if she was to retain any semblance of sanity. Funny how she had to fight with herself to say the word.

'N-no.'

Silence.

'You mean, you won't even consider it?' Hamish asked at last.

'That's what. . . That's what I said. No.' Lilly pulled back against Hamish's grip but she wasn't released.

'Why not, Lilly?'

Because you don't love me, her heart was screaming. Because you don't want me as I want to be wanted. You don't love me as I want to be loved.

She couldn't tell him that. Heaven knew, she'd thrown herself at him once as a lovesick student. She wasn't throwing herself at him again today.

'Because. . .' Lilly shook her head, hardly knowing

herself why she was shaking it. 'Because I want more from a marriage than that, Hamish. What I want. . . Well, five years ago I thought I'd found what I wanted with you. I was wrong. Stupid. But it hasn't stopped me hoping. That one day. . .one day I'll feel again like I did then. That I can give my heart. . .'

How much more could she say?

Could she say that she had already given her heart? Once—five years ago? She'd told him she loved him then—and he'd assumed that she'd somehow stopped. Somehow stopped loving. . . She hadn't. Her heart belonged absolutely to this man. And if she told him again. . . If she told him then he'd smile that gentle smile and take her into his arms and take her as his wife.

Problem solved.

Angus satisfied. Davey fathered.

And Lilly?

Lilly befriended. Made a wife to a man who'd already had a wife. He'd married once in passion. This was his second try and it wasn't to be the same. It was to be a marriage of convenience.

OK, Hamish's marriage to Lauris had ended in disaster, but at least there had once been passion. And he wasn't offering Lilly the same terms even at the start of this marriage contract.

She couldn't bear it.

'You couldn't give your heart to me—again?' Hamish asked gently and Lilly's eyes filled with stupid, unwanted tears.

Hamish the teacher. Lilly the silly, immature student. Giving her heart to a man who would care for it like some pretty ornament to be placed on a shelf and tended—but not used. Not joined to his so closely it could never be torn asunder.

'I want a real marriage or nothing,' Lilly whispered. 'Hamish. . .I want the passion.'

There was a long, long silence.

Hamish looked as though he was taking what she had

said on board and turning it over and over in his mind.

And he was coming to some conclusion.

'Lilly, you don't think we could restart those fires?' Hamish asked finally. His hands were hot on her arms, as if they burned. His eyes searched hers and his hands gripped tighter. 'Lilly, look at me.'

'No.'

'Yes,' he ordered. 'Lilly, once you said you loved me.'

'Five years ago.' She couldn't meet those eyes. 'I was stupid.'

'Stupid?'

'Yes.'

'It didn't feel stupid then,' he said tightly and his voice had changed. There was a huskiness there now, and his expression had changed. His eyes were intent and penetrating—and dark with the beginning of something Lilly remembered from a long, long time ago. 'Lilly, I could start again—if that's what you want. . .'

Lilly didn't answer. She couldn't. She couldn't gather strength to have her mouth frame the words, much less make her voice operate at whisper level.

'Lilly, look at me.'

She did then—somehow. Hamish's dark eyes were on hers, his hands came up to push the damp curls back from her face—and his hands didn't drop again.

Instead they held her face—and brought it slowly forward to his.

And Lilly didn't resist. She couldn't fight this. There was no fight in her.

For five years Lilly had lived with the memory of this man's eyes—this man's hands—this man's body. Here was where she wanted to be. Two people melting into one. One body. One soul.

One heart.

She felt Hamish's warm, wide mouth touch her lips and a trail of fire started deep within. Her lips parted of their own accord as his kiss deepened, her mouth wanting him, welcoming him and her body aching with the need of five long, barren years.

Dear heaven. . .

She could think no further.

All that mattered now was that Hamish Campbell was kissing her as she wanted to be kissed. Holding her as she wanted to be held.

Taking her to him.

Her hands came up to touch his beloved face, holding him to her as fiercely as he held her.

She remembered his taste—his feel—his smell. Remembered? Wrong word! She didn't have to remember. Knowledge of this man had stayed with her all these long, long years. Part of her was his—had always been his—and her body knew it. She was responding to him now as if she was part of him, her bikini-clad body moving of its own accord so that she curled into him. Closer. Closer. . .

Somehow they were falling backward, off the outer ledge and back through onto the soft, sandy floor of the cave. Their lips were still linked and the flickering flame within Lilly's body were turning to white-hot need.

His hands were on her waist, pulling her in to him, pulling her breasts against his chest. Naked skin against naked skin. . . Damp body against damp body. . . It felt so right. . .

It felt so good.

It felt just as it had five years ago. When she hadn't known he was married. When she hadn't known that her world was going to fall apart.

The thought caught her—stabbing like a knife into Lilly's consciousness, hauling the flame back under control like a savage wall of ice water smashing into the linking lovers.

This man had made love to her, had wanted her, had made her feel like there was no one else in the world— and yet he hadn't loved her.

He'd never said he loved her.

He hadn't said it now.

Hamish was taking her now—making love to her now—because he wanted her. He wanted a wife. He wanted companionship and peace for his uncle. He wanted a partner in his medical practice and he wanted... he wanted her son.

No!

Somehow...

Somehow she forced herself to freeze within the tight circle of his arms. Somehow she made her body obey her mind's commands. Lilly turned rigid in Hamish's grasp.

Hamish felt her change and he pulled back so that their eyes were six inches apart in the filtered light of the little cave.

'What is it, Lilly?'

His voice was husky with passion and his hands still held her naked waist. Her body was curled into his and she could still feel what was between them... She could feel his arousal.

No! She was out of her mind, doing this!

With a savage shove Lilly pushed herself back, breaking the one into two again.

'No!'

It was a cry of terror.

Hamish could hear the fear in Lilly's voice and his brow creased into a frown. His long, surgeon's fingers came up to stroke her hair in what was meant as a gesture of reassurance, but Lilly shoved his hand away with fear.

This man could manipulate her to do anything he wanted. With this man her body was out of control.

She had to be out of her mind! What on earth was she doing here? She was lying almost naked with Hamish Campbell.

In minutes... Feeling like they did, in minutes he'd

have her completely naked and she'd be past the point of pulling back.

You stupid fool, Lilly, she screamed silently at herself. She'd taken no precautions. For heaven's sake, Hamish Campbell could well make her pregnant all over again.

Her behaviour here was no better than the immature teenagers she counselled about the dangers of unplanned sex, she told herself savagely, fighting the feeling Hamish's hands on her body was causing. Maybe her behaviour was even more stupid. She'd been caught once. Made pregnant. . . She knew the heartbreak and loneliness that followed.

She'd be a fool to give herself to this man again.

Not ever.

'Let. . . Hamish, let me go.'

Somehow she dragged herself back from him, back out to the ledge. This place was too small. She couldn't get away from him here.

There was only one option. Before he could protest, Lilly had shoved herself off the ledge and was letting the waterfall pound her under, out and back into the safety of the open pool.

Hamish followed.

He surfaced ten seconds after Lilly did and the two of them trod water for a long moment as they regained their breath.

'Lilly. . .' Hamish regained his voice first. He was six feet from her in the water. She stared wildly across at him, her breathing coming in shallow gasps and her breasts heaving with combined anger and panic.

He reached for her in the water but she shoved herself back from him, glaring like a tiger defending its young.

'Get away from me.' Out here she had to yell to make herself heard above the force of the water, but somehow she managed it.

'What the hell. . .?' He didn't try to follow. 'Lilly, I thought you wanted. . .'

'You thought I wanted you to make love to me? You have to be kidding!'

'You wanted it as much as I did,' he growled. 'Lilly, your body wanted me.'

'Yeah!' She was yelling at the top of her lungs now, half because she had to to make herself heard and because she wanted to. Half because she was so angry that she thought she'd burst.

Or cry.

'My body might have wanted it,' she yelled. 'Just like it always has. You can make love to me and make me forget what I should remember and I'm almost as stupid as I was five years ago. But I'm not. I'd rather die than take what you're offering, Hamish Campbell.

'Marriage! A marriage of convenience to supply a partner and a mother and a companion. . .I wouldn't be the least bit surprised if you suggest sacking Mrs Price so you get a housekeeper in the package as well. But I'm not a raw, green student any longer, Hamish Campbell. I'm me. Independent doctor. Lilly Inger— wife of no man and convenience of no one. And I'm going home. Now. I'm taking the car and if you don't come you can walk.'

'Lilly, I didn't mean. . .'

'I don't care what you meant,' she sobbed in mingled humiliation and rage. How could she have let this happen? How could she? 'I'm leaving here at the end of the week, Hamish Campbell, and if you don't like it you can lump it. And I'd just as soon you lumped it!'

CHAPTER TEN

LILLY dressed and drove home beside Hamish in silent, fuming rage.

How dared Hamish Campbell treat her like this? How dared he?

She sat and glowered at the road ahead and only a tiny voice whispered the truth into an inner ear. That as soon as the anger faded she was going to burst into tears.

Marriage to Hamish. A marriage to suit all concerned—a neat solution, with Hamish producing passion if she required it. Producing friendship if she required it. What sort of crazy marriage would that be?

Better than no marriage at all, another voice whispered, but her heart knew better. Lilly's heart knew which way heartbreak lay. It lay all around her—whether she married Hamish Campbell or not—and at least by leaving. . . At least by leaving there would be moments when she could forget him.

Maybe.

She sat and glowered some more. Hamish glanced at her from time to time, but her rigid pose, her folded arms and her thunderous face kept him silent.

Except for once.

'You know you look like the avenging angel,' he commented once, his mouth curving into a suspicion of a grin—and Lilly gasped and fought hard to stay glowering.

All she wanted was to get home—to get back to Davey and the sanctuary of a good howling pillow—and when Hamish steered off the main road before the doctor's residence she forced herself to break the silence.

'Where are we going?' she demanded.

155

'There's no need to sound so suspicious,' Hamish said gently. 'I'm not planning on making a bolt for Gretna Green, with you chained to the passenger seat. It's a bit far and a bit wet, even for a car as good as this.'

Lilly gasped and sharpened her glare.

'I want to go home, Hamish Campbell.'

'So do I, Lilly.' Hamish shrugged. 'But I want to find Steven Carter first and I thought it might be better if we both faced him. The boy has some explaining to do and if he admits giving Claire drugs, then I want a witness. It's either you or the police sergeant, and you're not quite as threatening.'

'Oh.' Lilly subsided to a silent fume. There was no argument to his logic, but she didn't have to like it.

Steven Carter wasn't at home and his mother appeared at the door with concern etched over her kindly, middle-aged face.

'Oh, Dr Campbell. . .' She seized Hamish's hand and practically wrung it. 'No, I don't know where Steven is and I'm that worried. . .'

'I thought he'd be home from cricket by now,' Hamish frowned.

'He didn't go to cricket. The team captain rang me up and asked where the heck Steven was. They were depending on him to show because it was an important match.' Her eyes filled with tears. 'And I'm that worried. I know what happened last night. Claire was ill and Steven reckoned she'd taken something she shouldn't have and he was so scared. He felt responsible, you see—convincing her parents to let her go to the party and all—'

'Did Steven stay with Claire all night?' Hamish asked and Mrs Carter shook her head.

'He wouldn't.' She wiped her eyes. 'He told me about it at breakfast—said Claire was crook and behaving funny and Debbie said she ought to stay at her place so they propped Claire up while she rang her parents. And Steven came back here and went back after breakfast to get her and drive her home. Only. . . He came back here afterwards. Said Claire was weird and he was that frightened.

'He came back again after he drove her home and he seemed scared—but he also seemed angry, Dr Campbell, like he knew what had happened and he wanted to knock someone down. And then he went off to work—he works Saturday mornings at the resort, and he hasn't come home again.'

Hamish nodded. 'How about letting Dr Inger make you a cup of tea, Mrs Carter?' he said gently. 'I'll do a bit of telephoning. Maybe it's time we found him.'

'Is Claire. . . Is Claire OK?'

'I rang Mr Burn ten minutes ago on my mobile phone,' Hamish said gently. 'Claire's sleeping soundly and looks like recovering.'

'From. . .from drugs?' Mrs Carter quavered and Hamish nodded.

'Yes, Mrs Carter. From drugs.'

They left the lady holding a rapidly cooling mug of tea and staring sightlessly in front of her. There was little they could say to comfort her until they found her son. Even then. . .

'I just hope to hell he didn't buy them and give them to her,' Hamish said savagely. 'He's a nice kid. They're both nice kids. Of all the stupid, senseless things to happen. . .'

'He seemed angry,' Lilly said mildly as their little car puttered back onto the main road. 'It points to him not being responsible himself but knowing who is.'

'Or him being misinformed as to the drug's side-effects,' Hamish growled. 'Dealers play down risks. They might have sold the stuff to Steven and told him it'd make Claire an easy target—without warning him that it also might make her really ill. Where the hell is the kid?'

'He couldn't have panicked and run?' Lilly wondered. Her fuming had to be put aside for the time
being. Hamish was in no mood to notice, no matter
how hard she glowered. 'Could he have caught the ferry
to the mainland?'

'That was one of the phone calls I made,' Hamish
told her. 'The ferry-master tells me he hasn't seen
Steven today. I also rang the resort. The receptionist
says Steven reported for work this morning but she
hasn't seen him round this afternoon. There are a couple
of senior groundsmen Steven works with. I thought we
could go and have a word with them now.'

He glanced across at Lilly. 'If you're not too angry
to come with me.'

Lilly pursed her lips. 'I'm not angry,' she muttered.

His eyes creased in a rueful smile. 'Yeah? And my
name's not Hamish Campbell.'

Steven wasn't at the resort, but once again they found
someone worried for his welfare. The head groundsman
was Pete Roe, a ferret-faced little man with skin like
leather. He greeted them with something akin to relief
when the receptionist directed them to where the head
gardener was working.

'Yeah. He's been here. Sick as a dog, too, and I don't
mean sick in the stomach,' Pete told them. 'Just upset
as I've ever seen him—and angry. Bloody furious. I
put him to digging some of his anger off in the new
fernery but he'd only been here half an hour when Mr
Oswald came out and took him away with him.'

'Mr Oswald?' Lilly queried and Hamish grimaced.

'Owen Oswald. Resort manager,' he told her and
Lilly grimaced too. Oil-Head.

'Do you know where they went?' Hamish asked and
the gardener scratched his head.

'I dunno where they are but I know where they were,'
he told them. 'Mr Oswald took Steve into the bar and
gave him a drink or two. Or three or four by the look

of it. Funny, that. Mr Oswald's not the man to be buying his employees drinks. Maybe he saw Steve was upset.' He scratched his head again. 'But it's still funny. . .' He sighed and picked up his hoe again. 'Ask the barman. Maybe Dan'll know where they went.'

Dan didn't.

'But I reckon—maybe Mr Oswald took him home,' the barman suggested helpfully. 'He sure couldn't drive himself.'

'Why not?'

'Because he's had a skinful,' Dan said roundly. 'Steve's not a kid who's used to much drink—especially spirits. He came in here upset and Mr Oswald gave him a double whisky and then told me to keep his glass filled.' He frowned. 'Seemed like a stupid way to comfort the kid, if you ask me—but Mr Oswald's my boss and he's not one to take criticism kindly.'

'When did they leave?' Lilly asked, as Hamish frowned down at the brilliantly polished mahogany bar. The place was still deserted after the diphtheria scare and with its fabulous interior design and the view of the ocean stretching for ever out the full length windows the place seemed more a movie set than a real-life bar.

'About half an hour ago,' the barman said helpfully. 'As I said, I didn't see them go but if that's what happened then I reckon Mr Oswald will have him safely home with his mum by now.'

'Only he hasn't,' Hamish said grimly as they re-emerged into daylight. 'We would have passed them on the road. Lilly, I'm starting to get a few really bad feelings about all of this. What the hell's Owen Oswald playing at?'

'Comforting a worried employee?' Lilly said softly and Hamish gave a derisive laugh.

'You've met the man, Lilly. What do you think?'

'I think,' Lilly said carefully, 'I think Owen Oswald wouldn't give you the time of day unless there was something in it for Owen Oswald.'

'Right,' Hamish snapped. He lifted his mobile phone and stood staring out to sea as he dialled—firstly the operator for the number and then Mrs Fraser. Debbie's mother, Mrs Fraser, was hostess of last night's disastrous party.

'Mrs Fraser? Dr Campbell here. No, no, I'm not ringing about Claire. Claire's recovering. I rang to ask about something else. Mrs Fraser, was the manager of the resort—Owen Oswald—at Debbie's party last night? He was? How long? Oh, I see. Yes, it was very kind of him to bother. Thanks, Mrs Fraser. Thanks for your help.'

Hamish snapped the phone shut and his face tightened.

'Debbie Fraser's a part-time waitress at the resort,' he told Lilly. 'According to Mrs Fraser, Owen Oswald popped in to the party for an hour or two—just to be sociable. Debbie was pleased as Punch because she wants to leave school and get a full-time job here. She thought he came because he liked her.'

'And you think he came because. . .'

'I'm guessing,' Hamish said slowly. 'I can't prove a thing. But suppose. . . Just suppose Owen Oswald is the drug dealer on this island. He could well be the dealer for most of the nearby mainland, too. Wayne Reid has been on the island a lot lately. Let's assume Owen pushes the drugs through him. Only Wayne gets addicted and unreliable and finally gets himself arrested. At the same time, the resort suffers the diphtheria scare and funds from there dry up.'

'But. . .' Lilly frowned. 'If Owen's the manager he'll be on a salary. It shouldn't affect him.'

'Owen tells everyone here he's only the manager but I've heard on the grapevine he's invested his own money in it,' Hamish told her, thinking aloud. 'And the resort hasn't been doing too well lately. So he's had a week of no hotel income and no drug income and maybe—just maybe—there's another drug drop due.

'This place would be ideal to use for offloading drugs from foreign ships as they come through toward Sydney. Customs can't keep their eye on every small island.

'But if a shipment's due—then Owen will need ready cash and he's short. Answer—he has to deal the drugs himself for a week or so. I know there are drug-dependent kids on the island already. He'll supply them. But he gets a bit greedy. So... While he's at the party why not see if he can drum up a few future customers? And he talks silly little Claire into trying LSD.'

'And maybe... Maybe Steven saw, or Claire told Steven what happened when he took her home this morning,' Lilly said slowly.

'And Steven's fighting mad—but he wouldn't go to the police because he thinks he'll get Claire into trouble. So he goes to work—and confronts Owen.'

Lilly bit her lip. 'So now... Now what...?'

'I don't know,' Hamish muttered. He lifted his phone again. 'I'll ring the police for a start. It's time we got them involved. And then...' He stared out to sea. 'If you were Owen... If you were someone who thought Steven Carter could blow the whistle on your whole little operation... And you've got him blind drunk... What would you do to him?'

They both knew the answer. And neither of them liked it one bit.

By the time Hamish finished his short telephone conversation with the police sergeant, both Lilly's and Hamish's expressions showed clearly what each was thinking.

'He wouldn't dare,' Lilly whispered, but she didn't believe it for a moment. She'd worked with drug addicts in the past. Addicts themselves were fearful enough but the dealers were worse. Their massive incomes depended on addicting enough victims to keep their fortunes intact. Honour among thieves? Maybe, but there was no honour among drug dealers.

'If Steven was drunk and then was found dead of a drug overdose—we wouldn't be able to prove a thing,' Hamish said grimly.

'So we need to find him before Owen. . .before Owen hurts him,' Lilly whispered. 'Hamish, where would he take him? He'd want to take him somewhere he wouldn't be found until he was well and truly dead. But it'd have to be somewhere Steven might go himself. It'd have to look like Steven crawled away to shoot up—or commit suicide.'

Hamish was silent, his face as grim as death. The warm sea breeze swept gently around them and the beauty of the ocean seemed almost an obscenity in the midst of this life and death drama.

'It'd have to be close enough for him to get back here fast. There are dozens of places. . .' And then Hamish froze in mid-sentence. 'But. . .'

'But?'

'The camp, Lilly. The camp at Turtle Point, where the group with diphtheria were staying.'

'But. . .' Lilly stared. Was it possible?

The more she thought about it the more it seemed not only possible but probable. The place had been sealed for all the previous week and was to be sealed for another week yet. All but superficial cleaning—removal of belongings and perishable foodstuffs—had been left. It was safer to let diphtheria germs die in their own time rather than launder sheets and clean floors when diphtheria bugs might still be active.

'But Owen will be afraid of the diphtheria.'

'Not him.' Hamish said grimly. 'He's up to date with his inoculations. He told me that when we were arranging for the hotel guests to be tested.' His mouth tightened. 'It fits. If the man's been fetching drugs from outlandish places—or dealing with people who have been overseas a lot—he'd worry about inoculations.'

'So?' Lilly asked slowly. 'Do we wait for the police?'

'I'll have the sergeant meet us there,' Hamish told

her, already moving quickly toward the car. 'If Owen's doing what I fear he's doing there's no time.' He looked round the car park, searching for faster transport, but there was only one car still in sight. Angus's Model T. It was that or nothing.

'I hope to heck it's built for rally driving,' Hamish muttered as he ran. 'Let's go, Lilly.'

The old car did them proud, putting on a turn of speed that might well have given Angus another heart attack if he'd known how his beloved baby was being treated. There was no time now for consideration of the delicate innards of vintage cars. There was only Steven's life.

Lilly shoved aside the barricades along the road, leaping down to the road every time Hamish slowed and climbing back into the car with a sense of urgency that only increased the nearer they got to Turtle Point.

Their urgency was justified. They found Steven, just in time. Steven was very, very close to death.

Hamish found him. He'd broken into the first villa as Lilly ran to the second but Hamish's urgent yell had her racing back.

There was no trace of Owen Oswald but at least— at least they'd found Steven.

The boy lay limp and huddled on an unmade bed, his body looking as if it had been tossed there rather than placed with care. His arms were sprawled out and he reeked of alcohol.

It wasn't alcohol that was doing the damage now. Steven's breathing was so shallow as to be close to non-existent—indeed, Lilly's first thought was that they were too late—but Hamish was ripping the boy's shirt away and frantically searching Steven's tanned arms.

He found what he was looking for in seconds.

'The bastard!' he said grimly. 'We were right, Lilly. Here are fresh needle marks. He'll have injected heroin, at a guess, and heaven knows how much. We'll have to assume the worst. Lilly, get my bag—fast!'

Lilly's feet were already flying.

In seconds she was back, hauling open the bag and searching for the naloxone, intravenous catheter, fluids and tubing even before she'd stopped running. This was second nature, her casualty department training coming to the fore. When addicts were brought in unconscious with overdoses the first action was to set up a drip, administer the antidote fast—and hope and hope and hope!

So she hoped. Lilly thought fleetingly back to this boy's kindly, worried mother and her heart stirred in pity. Oil-Head had a lot to answer for.

Maybe he didn't have a death yet though. Not with a doctor of Hamish Campbell's skill. Lilly assisted as Hamish found the vein in the back of the boy's hand and carefully inserted the catheter for the drip. He didn't hesitate. There was no questioning this man's skill, and Steven's life depended on it.

The emotional see-saw of the afternoon might never have happened between Hamish and Lilly. Conflict between the two doctors was forgotten totally as they worked together to get the drip going at maximum flow. The boy was so close to death. . .

'I suppose. . .I suppose Owen must have done this,' Lilly murmured as they worked. 'Steven couldn't have done this himself.'

'It'll be impossible to prove,' Hamish said darkly, adjusting the mask on Steven's face and turning him slightly on his side to help his fragile breathing. 'If Steven dies. . . Well, Steven is drunk—what's the bet his blood alcohol is up to around point two or more?—and the jury would be asked to believe Owen murdered him in cold blood. There's no proof it was Owen. We didn't see him here.'

'No.'

'But if we get him back. . .' Hamish picked up Steven's lifeless hand and held it hard, as if he was trying to impart life with his strength. 'If we manage to keep him alive. . . He must have seen Owen supply Claire. . . There's no other explanation as to why Owen would have panicked this much.'

Lilly nodded.

They fell silent then, observing Steven together as they willed the naloxone to work.

Once—for two endless minutes—his breathing failed completely and they used artificial resuscitation to get him back.

But at last the antidote took hold.

The change in Steven's breathing was almost imperceptible in the beginning but finally, finally, the colour drifted slowly back into the boy's face and the worst of the peril seemed over.

'OK.' Hamish stood back from the bed, his breathing as heavy as Steven's was shallow. Resuscitation was sheer physical effort. 'Let's get him into the clinic before the effects of the antidote wear off.'

Lilly nodded. It was often necessary to re-administer the naloxone every few minutes or so because the effect of heroin lasted longer than the antidote. Steven was by no means out of the woods yet.

Hamish looked round at the still-open villa door as the sound of the police car's siren cut across the gentler sound of the surf.

'Here's the police sergeant.' He grunted in relief. He lifted the unconscious boy's hand. 'OK, Steven, let's get you safe and then see if we can pick up Owen Oswald.' His face darkened. 'Proof or not, he has a hell of a lot of explaining to do.'

Steven was transported to the clinic in the back of the police car, Hamish with him and Lilly travelling behind in Angus's car. The Model T Ford was hardly useful as an ambulance, she thought regretfully.

What would happen now? What would happen to Steven? The urgency was gone. The removal of crises left her limp and drained—and not at all sure that she wanted to keep following the police car home.

Hamish could cope by himself now. He didn't need her. Too much had happened too fast. Her tired mind couldn't take it all in.

Lilly thought of Claire lying back in the farmhouse bedroom, not knowing the dangers her boyfriend had put himself through on her account. Steven must love her, she thought drearily.

Lucky Claire.

You're feeling sorry for yourself, she told herself savagely as her thoughts drifted. For heaven's sake, you have much more than Claire Burn. She's in a mess and you're not.

Oh yes, you are, a little voice whispered in the back of her mind and she couldn't deny it.

The events of the last hour had shifted her thoughts from what was happening between Hamish and herself. In some ways it had given her a respite but now, driving by herself back to the house and with Steven safely in another doctor's care, the enotions of what had happened at the waterfall came flooding back.

Yes, she was in a mess. Because she was in love with a man who had lost the capacity to return that love.

She'd have to face it.

Hamish had been serious when he'd asked her to marry him. She had no doubt that if she'd said yes then she'd end up as his wife.

His wife of convenience.

Well, he'd just have to stop being serious, she thought savagely. If he caught her at a weak moment before she managed to leave the island. . .

Lilly glanced out at the ocean, which was starting to turn dusky pink now with the reflected rays of the setting sun. Nooluk had become her home so rapidly. She was learning to care so quickly—for the island kids like Claire and Steven, as well as for Angus and Mrs Price—and Hamish. . .

She had to get out of here. She had to leave fast. This place was like a spider's web, catching her in its sticky trap and drawing her in tighter the more she struggled.

CHAPTER ELEVEN

THERE was little time in the next two hours for contemplating her future.

Hamish took over Steven's care in the clinic and Lilly went straight to afternoon surgery.

Saturday's surgery patients were waiting placidly. They'd been there since five and it was now seven but the islanders had learned long ago to wait with patience if it was one of their own who was ill. Heaven knows how they'd found out that Steven and Claire were in trouble, but they knew and Lilly was interrogated before every patient's consultation as to the welfare of the two teenagers.

Hamish and the island's chief nursing sister were fully occupied with Steven, but an hour after his admission to the clinic Hamish rang through to the surgery and told Lilly that he was out of danger.

'Steven's still drifting in and out of unconsciousness and is incoherent,' he told her. 'The alcohol alone would have made him like that but, with luck, he'll be fit enough to tell us what happened by morning.'

'And. . .and Owen Oswald?'

'The police haven't been able to find him,' Hamish replied. 'He can't have left the island unless he had access to a boat we didn't know about. The police sergeant is checking all boat operators now.'

'But if he disappears he'll lose everything,' Lilly frowned. 'Would he run for it? Just walk away from the hotel and everything he owns?'

'He must be pretty darned worried to do that,' Hamish said reflectively. 'But it does depend completely on Steven and what he can tell us. Only Oswald can tell us what that is until Steven's conscious again.

'I've been on the phone to Claire's parents. Claire's awake and sensible—but she won't say a word of what happened last night. Says there must have been something in her drink or in the food to make her ill. Claire's mum says she seems scared stiff—as if she's been threatened with something dire if she tells the truth.'

'So there's only Steven,' Lilly said slowly. 'Well, let's hope he remembers.'

'And how about you, Lilly?' Hamish asked gently, cutting across her thoughts. 'Are you coping OK with surgery?'

Hamish's sudden change of tone and subject caught Lilly by surprise and she flushed.

'Yes. . . Thank you. I. . . Why shouldn't I be?'

She heard a smile come into his voice. 'There's no need to sound prickly,' the voice on the other end of the phone teased. 'I just thought you might be tired again. It's a whole six hours now since you had a sleep.'

'Hmm!' Lilly replaced the phone with an indignant swipe and tried to suppress an answering smile.

Hamish's laughter was contagious.

So was everything about Hamish Campbell. The man was as more-ish as a block of chocolate.

Or a whole sweet shop!

After surgery Lilly went across to the clinic—the east wing of their big house—to check on Steven for herself. Hamish was alone, coping with bookwork at a desk six feet from Steven's screened bed. He looked up as Lilly entered and put a finger to his lips.

'Shh.'

'What are you doing here alone?' Lilly asked, frowning. 'Isn't there a nurse for night duty?'

'There is,' Hamish agreed, 'but I'm not happy about her staying here by herself. I thought I'd stay here until midnight and then the local policeman's going to come back and keep watch while Sister returns to look after Steven's medical needs until morning. Sergeant Grey's running a few local checks to try and locate Oswald now.'

'Is there only one policeman on the island?' Lilly asked uneasily and Hamish nodded.

'It's a quiet island. One policeman's normally all we need. If we need another then headquarters sends someone over from the mainland—but we haven't been able to justify anyone else tonight.' Hamish shrugged. 'After all, as far as the authorities are concerned there's been no crime committed. Not until Steven talks.'

'So you think...you think someone might try and get at Steven. Owen might come...'

Lilly looked round the dimly lit room and shivered.

'I'm sure he won't,' Hamish smiled reassuringly. 'I've left all the outside lights on and and the windows open. If he comes he can see me here clearly—and we've put a screen up so the bed's hidden from view. So he can't see Steven and he can see me.'

'And that should be enough to strike terror into the heart of any criminal,' Lilly said sarcastically and Hamish nodded.

'That's the idea.' He rose and flexed a white-coated bicep. 'What do you think, Lilly?'

'I think you're perfectly ridiculous,' she said crossly.

He stood looking down at her in the dim light. His face stilled.

'And I think you're perfectly beautiful, Lillian Inger,' he said at last. 'You haven't reconsidered...?'

'No, I have not!' Lilly backed away like a startled rabbit, moving fast toward the door. 'Hamish, no...'

'You mean you don't want me don't propose again?' he asked and his smile faded completely.

'That's just what I do mean.'

There was a long, long silence. They looked at each other in the soft light thrown from the desk lamp, unanswered questions flowing back and forth—unspoken but tangible, for all that.

One of them had to move—but neither did.

In the end it was Steven who broke the deadlock. The boy in the bed behind the screen stirred and moaned—and Hamish turned.

The spell was broken.

'I'll. . .I'll go,' Lilly said. 'If there's nothing you need me for.'

'I do need you,' Hamish said softly, glancing back at her white face. 'You must know that.'

'I meant. . .I meant now.' Lilly's voice was bordering on desperate. 'Ham. . . Dr Campbell, is there anything you want me to do right now?'

'I guess there's not,' Hamish told her softly, his voice growing grim. He started to load a syringe, his back to her and all his attention now on the job at hand. 'I guess you can go to bed, Lilly. For now you're right. I don't need you.'

Lilly made her way slowly upstairs through a darkened house.

It was time to go to bed.

To sleep? There was as little chance of sleep for Lilly Inger that night as there was for. . .as there was for Owen Oswald.

Somewhere out there the man was trying to figure out his next move, Lilly thought bleakly. Could Steven give enough evidence to have him put behind bars?

She gave an involuntary shiver and went in to check Davey.

The child was fast asleep. For a while Lilly sat beside her small son, content to watch the gentle rise and fall of his chest and his innocent little face against the pillow.

Edward was hugged tightly under one arm. The two were now inseparable and at the sight of nose against nose Lilly felt a lump rise in her throat that threatened to choke her.

Why was nothing simple? Why did her life have to be so complicated and so. . .so unfair?

Finally, in a last attempt to shake off her morbid

thoughts, she made her way along the passage to Angus McVie's bedroom. There was a chink of light showing under his door and she knocked and entered.

The old man was sitting up in bed in his purple pyjamas, reading a paperback with a rather lurid cover. As Lilly opened the door he shoved the book down under the covers and blushed deep crimson.

'Oh-ho,' Lilly chuckled, her bleak mood fading. 'So our Dr McVie has a vice, has he? I knew the image of sainted country doctor was too good to be true.'

'It's an educational text,' Angus McVie grinned at her. His colour deepened but he managed to meet her eyes squarely. 'Family counselling. . .'

'Oh, yeah?' Lilly grinned. 'What to do if you're a randy male and your family happens to be a dozen or so nymphettes?'

'Only two nymphettes as it happens,' Angus smiled. 'And, believe me, it's very educational.' He propped himself up further and his smile faded. 'What's happening downstairs, lass?'

It couldn't hurt to tell him. If Angus McVie felt excluded he'd only fret—or hike downstairs to the clinic to see for himself—so Lilly pulled up a chair and recounted the gist of the day's events. The episode at the waterfall she carefully excluded.

Angus listened in grim silence, thought for a while in silence as Lilly finished the story and then finally nodded.

'I don't doubt you're right, lass,' he said slowly. 'I never liked that Oswald. Too smooth by half—and inclined to treat the medical service like servants who should be delighted to be summoned by the likes of him.' He frowned. 'You say he's still on the island, though. Is Steven safe in the clinic?'

'The police sergeant's coming back at midnight,' Lilly said solidly—more solidly than she felt. Part of her would like to take herself downstairs and sit with Hamish—and part of her wasn't game.

And it wasn't fear of Owen Oswald. It was fear of sitting in a dim room for an hour or more—with Hamish.

'Why don't you go downstairs until then?' Angus said quietly, watching her face. 'It's what you want to do, isn't it girl?'

'I don't. . .I don't. . .'

'Has he asked you to marry him yet?'

The question was so blunt that it took Lilly's breath away.

'Angus. . .'

'If he hasn't yet the man's a fool.' Angus McVie peered more closely at her white face. 'But I'd be thinking he has popped the question, hasn't he, lass? And by the look of your face, you're refusing the man.'

'Dr McVie, this is none of your business,' Lilly said desperately.

'There was a time I would have said you're right,' Angus told her, his kindly eyes never leaving hers. 'But I'm seventy-five years old, girl, and I've watched my nephew mess his life round for too damned long. The boy does the right thing—always. He did the right thing by that no-good wife of his. He's done the right thing by me.

'And now. . . Now he won't put pressure on you because he thinks he's wronged you—and if he doesn't stop doing the right thing soon I won't live to see a happy ending. And I'm big on happy endings.'

Lilly fell silent. How much of this was the truth? Hamish refusing to pressure her because it wasn't the right thing to do. . .

'Well, girl?' Angus growled. 'Are you planning on giving me a happy ending? Curing me with a bridal remedy rather than stuff like anginine and these nuisance GTN patches?'

'Do your nymphettes have a happy ending?' Lilly managed, trying her hardest to change the subject.

'I'll just bet they do,' Angus said roundly. 'This

author's an author I can depend on. The lad'll walk down the aisle with a lady on each arm before the story's out. Wedding cake and champagne for all and then a wedding night to make a man's blood pressure rise. I might have to skip the last few pages in deference to my weak heart.' His smile faded. 'But our Hamish doesn't want more than one lady. He only wants you.'

'He only wants Davey,' Lilly said bitterly and then wished she hadn't.

The old man stiffened. He was staring at her in round-eyed amazement.

'He only wants Davey. . .' Is that what he said?'

'It's what he meant.'

'That's nonsense.'

'It isn't,' Lilly said quietly. 'He wants to marry me to keep you happy and to keep Davey on the island.'

'He wants to marry you because he hasn't been able to think of any other woman for five long years,' Angus told her. He lifted his paperback from under the covers and smiled ruefully down at the torrid cover.

'I should know. The boy takes after me. I met my wife fifty years ago, she's been dead ten years and, paperback beauties aside, I've never thought of another. Not since the day I set my eyes on my Lillian.' He looked up as Lilly's eyes widened and his smile grew distant.

'That's right, lass. She had the same name as yours and she was every bit as beautiful. A woman in a million. And Hamish found his woman in a million when he found you, and you're all he wants—all he's ever wanted—and if he can't say that to you because of his damned scruples then it's time someone said it for him.'

'How. . .how do you know?' Lilly whispered.

'Because he's told me,' Angus said. 'It was true his mother told me about you, but I had first-hand sources of my own. He told me himself, here, in this very room.

'Hamish came to the island when I had my first coronary and told me he was coming here to live and

I said "Don't be stupid. You're cutting yourself off from the world. Lauris is dead but there are other women out there. Stay where you can have a decent social life. Give yourself a chance." And you know what he said?'

'N-no.'

'He said he'd met his lady. He said he'd met a woman when Lauris was alive and she was everything he'd ever dreamed of. Said he'd treated her so badly she never wanted to see him again, and he deserved her scorn—but he still carried her in his heart.' Angus shrugged.

'It's the sort of talking that's only possible between a nephew and uncle when the nephew thinks the uncle is close to death and pretence has no place. And then I recovered—and maybe he thought I'd forgotten. But I hadn't. Because I know how he feels—like I feel about my Lillian. My own Lilly.'

Lilly's eyes had filled with tears. She shook her head blindly. 'Dr McVie. . .I don't know. . . He doesn't say. . .'

'Then maybe it's time for you to say it for him,' Angus McVie said roughly. 'You're the one wronged. He thinks he's hurt you past forgiveness. If you want him. . .if you love him. . .then maybe you have the courage enough to step through pride.' He smiled.

'If it was my Lillian. . . I met my Lilly when I was a young medical student. I had nothing, and I had three years' study ahead of me before I could think of supporting a wife. My Lilly's parents wanted her to marry a local storekeeper—a man with substance. So. . .I did the right thing and walked away—and Lillian walked right after me. I found her camped by the door of my lodgings and she declared she was staying there until I married her.'

Angus reached out and took Lilly's hand. 'So I married her and I loved her for ever. Pride and love don't mix, lass. You know that. Now...what are you going to do about it?'

Lilly didn't answer. She couldn't. Tears were slipping down her face so fast that she was blinded and she twisted away in pain.

'If I thought... If I thought you were right...'

'I am right,' Angus said bluntly. 'You go down to him now. And give him half a chance, lass. The boy's hot-blooded enough. I reckon half a chance is all he needs.'

Lilly didn't go downstairs straight away.

She crept back to her bedroom and stood for what seemed an age staring out her bedroom window at the moonlit sea.

Was Angus right?

Hamish had kept her photograph all these years. She knew that.

And what had been between them once had been like gold. A feeling so sweet it was beyond description. She had felt that—and here was Angus saying that Hamish felt it too.

She'd never know—unless she exposed her own feelings.

Maybe Hamish would say that he still loved her to persuade her to marry him. To have permanent access to his son.

Hamish didn't lie. She knew that.

Hamish was a man of honour...

Why hadn't he said he still loved her?

She turned the thought over and over in her mind and the answer was crystal clear. Hamish still thought of her as that wide-eyed student from years ago. He'd think of declarations of love and dependence as emotional blackmail. Unfair pressure...

'Honourable fool,' she whispered and a wry little smile played around her mouth. Hamish was no fool. He was the most intelligent, most caring...most loving...

'Give him half a chance, lass,' Angus had said. 'Half a chance is all he needs. . .'

It wouldn't hurt to go down. To repair the ravages of her face and walk downstairs and see. . .see what happened.

She turned from the window—and then froze. As she'd glanced downward in turning, she'd thought she'd seen something.

She was right. There was someone in the shrubbery below the house. Someone moving stealthily toward the lighted window of the clinic. Where Hamish sat by Steven. . .

Lilly's feet were moving almost before she realised what she had seen, flying out of the door and stumbling down the stairs. Hamish. . . Hamish was sitting by the lighted window.

And she'd seen something more that had made her blood freeze in horror. The furtive figure held something in his hand and, as he'd moved, the moonlight had glinted on metal. He was too far away for her to be sure—but the sight of metal in a hand was enough.

There was only one horrible conclusion.

It took thirty dreadful seconds for Lilly reach the clinic door.

Lilly didn't scream. Screaming here was useless. Hamish had told her that they'd had the dividing walls soundproofed to separate the house from the clinic's noise—or vice versa—as much as they could. Lilly could have picked up the phone and dialled—but the phone was downstairs anyway and it was faster to run.

The hall floor was polished wood and Lilly slipped, wasting three precious seconds. Then she was up again, scrambling to her feet and tearing along the hall like a crazy woman. Propped near the front door was one of Angus's heavy walking canes and she grabbed it as she flew. Instinctive weapon against a loaded gun? Crazy, but Lilly was beyond thought.

Hamish, she was screaming in her head. Hamish. . .

She launched herself at the clinic door and burst through. . .

And stopped dead.

She was too late.

The clinic window was smashed and Hamish was sprawled back against the wall, one hand to his shoulder and his eyes wide and dazed with pain.

Even in the dim light Lilly could see blood.

And there was a man standing over him, lifting his gun again to aim. . . To aim straight for Hamish's heart.

What little control Lilly had left was gone completely as she somehow registered what was happening.

Her mad launch through the door didn't stop. She must have seemed the witch from hell to the two men, her heavy walking cane upraised, her mouth opening to scream and her body lifting in an automatic lunge at the man attacking her Hamish.

The man attacking her love.

The attacker with the gun whirled to face her, but Lilly was first. The cane rose high as she propelled herself at him and she brought it down with a force she didn't know she had—a force she could never possibly have again. The heavy wood crashed sickeningly into flesh, cracking and splintering with the massive force behind the blow, and the man crumpled where he stood.

Lilly didn't stop. The man sank to his knees, the gun lowered a little—but not enough—and the splintered cane smashed down again.

And again. . .

Hamish stopped her.

Somehow he managed to rise to his feet. He staggered over and his bloodied hand reached out to catch the cane.

'Enough, Lilly,' he said wearily. 'You'll kill the bastard. . .'

The effort was too much.

Hamish slumped to the floor, unconscious.

CHAPTER TWELVE

WITH the door dividing the clinic from the house flung wide by Lilly's mad rush, soundproofing was non-existent and aid arrived almost before Lilly could turn to help Hamish.

Mrs Price came first, rushing in without bothering to don her dressing-gown and standing stock-still in bare feet, nightie and curlers, surveying the chaos with horror.

Angus McVie was right behind her.

The elderly doctor, still resplendent in purple pyjamas, pushed Mrs Price out of the way without ceremony and knelt over Hamish. Blood was spurting from an artery in his shoulder. Lilly was trying to staunch the flow but her fingers wouldn't do what she ordered them to do. They were suddenly limp and lifeless.

'Out of the way, girl,' Angus growled. 'Get us a wad of lint. I need pressure here. Mrs Price, I suggest you phone the constabulary and then sit on our villain until the police arrive to deal with him. If he comes to, feel free to hit him again.' He looked reflectively at the remains of his walking-stick lying on the floor. 'You'll have to use a paperweight or some such, though. Our Lilly seems to have done a thorough job.'

'I think. . .' It was just as well that Angus's old hands were still skilful because Lilly was having trouble making anything work at all. The sight of Hamish lying unconscious was making her feel sick to the core. 'I think I killed him.'

'I doubt it, girl,' Angus growled. 'It'd take more than you to smash a head as thick as that. Not that you wouldn't be doing the community a service if you had.'

'But. . . But Hamish. . .'

179

'He'll live,' Angus told her decisively, deftly working on his nephew. 'The boy's pulse is still fine and nothing vital was in the bullet's path. I'm not saying he wouldn't have been poorly if he hadn't had help fast. He's lost too much blood but we can soon remedy that.' Amazingly, the frail old man seemed in his element. 'You'd better fetch me some plasma, girl, and some adrenaline. Look lively. I've had probationary nurses move faster than you.'

And then there seemed to be people everywhere.

Mrs Price's hysterical phone call seemed to produce not only the police sergeant but every able-bodied man on the island. Who knew what mayhem the housekeeper had described to the policeman but he'd certainly felt it necessary to call for back-up—and back-up arrived in force.

And then there were helicopters landing from the mainland and white-coated medicos, and Lilly and Angus were being edged kindly aside as trauma teams took over. The police had a conference in private and decided that everyone would be safer on the mainland— Steven and Hamish and the now-conscious and groaning Owen, and even Claire.

'We'll get them all where no one can get at any of them,' the superintendent from the mainland told Angus. 'I don't want to risk our Owen having any mates.'

Angus appeared very much in control. He stood directing operations with the authority of years, one arm round the still shaking Lilly.

He'd filled Hamish full of morphine and Hamish was drifting in and out of consciousness, weak with blood loss. Angus supervised as his nephew was loaded onto a stretcher and then he squeezed Lilly's waist and pushed her away from him.

'Go on, girl. Off you go with Hamish. You're not staying here.'

'But. . .' Lilly shook herself. 'I can't. . . Angus, I can't leave you.'

'If you don't leave me I promise to have another coronary on the spot,' he growled. 'Mrs Price and I will cope admirably by ourselves, won't we, Mrs Price?'

'We definitely will,' the housekeeper said roundly. She placed a hand on Lilly's arm. 'Go on, dear. I can take care of Davey and our Dr Angus. And Dr Hamish needs *you*.'

'Are you coming or not?' the head of the trauma team asked her, and suddenly there was no choice.

She couldn't leave Hamish alone.

Hamish woke at four in the morning.

They'd operated on arrival at Cairns, removing the fragments of lead from his shoulder and setting his shattered collar-bone.

'He's a lucky man,' the surgeon had told Lilly and she'd nodded blindly.

It wasn't only Hamish who was lucky.

She'd learned something in that blinding moment when Hamish had been facing the gun for the second time. Angus had said that there was no place for pride in love. Angus was right. There was no place for anything but love.

Lilly would give whatever it took.

The hospital had offered her a bed but Lilly had refused. Her place was by Hamish's side—for however long it took.

His eyes flickered open and she was there.

Lilly's hand was entwined in Hamish's larger one. She was in the recovery room. Usually at this stage there'd be a nurse beside the patient but in deference to Lilly's medical training they were left alone.

A nurse hovered in the background, but out of earshot.

'Welcome back,' Lilly smiled and bent and kissed him gently on the lips.

His eyes widened. 'Lilly. . .'

'I'm here.'

'Did you. . .?' His hand tightened on hers. 'Did you kill him?'

'I didn't even fracture his skull,' Lilly said disgustedly. 'Though I tried hard enough.'

'Rats,' he said and his lips curved in a faint smile as his eyes closed again. 'Stay.'

She didn't stay all night.

As Hamish drifted into natural slumber Lilly allowed herself to be persuaded to sleep as well. They gave her a small bedroom in the nurses' quarters. Some time around seven she woke. A phone call to Hamish's ward informed her that he also was awake—and asking whether her visit the night before had been a figment of his imagination.

She should go to him.

Not yet.

Lilly showered slowly and then decided to pay a brief visit to the infectious diseases ward, where all the diphtheria patients were in various stages of recovery.

The sight of Tommy breathing by himself was wonderful, and seeing Henry Gibbs with his wife almost let Lilly forget her inner turmoil. Henry was helping his wife eat breakfast, fussing like a hen with one chick. The pair greeted Lilly with beaming smiles and assurances that Margaret's heart seemed to have suffered no long-term damage and, as Lilly left, Henry's hand came out to take his wife's.

Clearly Henry Gibbs had decided to go with the strength.

Then—because she couldn't put it off any longer— Lilly finally made her way to Hamish's ward.

Hamish was in a room by himself. Lilly took three deep breaths, searching for courage.

It didn't come. A nurse was watching from Sister's station or else Lilly might have bolted for cover.

Go on, Lilly. You can do this.

What if I can't?

You can't back out now.

Three more breaths, and she knocked and entered—and found her love clad in hospital pyjamas, his left arm in a sling and the rest of him propped up in bed munching a piece of toast.

'Good grief,' she said faintly, absurdly shy.

Hamish looked down at his pyjamas and grinned. 'They're not that bad!'

'I meant...' Lilly managed a smile. 'I meant last time I saw you, you seemed at death's door.'

'I've a constitution like an ox,' he smiled across at her. He raised his toast in a right-handed salute and then placed it back on the plate. 'Lilly, come here.'

'Wh-why?'

'Because I'm not allowed out of bed yet,' he said patiently. 'In fact, the ox has rather shaky legs this morning—and only one arm. So he needs his lady to come within reaching distance.'

'What for?'

'Come here and I'll show you.'

Lilly swallowed. She looked across at that dangerous smile—those twinkling eyes—and her heart lurched in the same way it always had.

Nothing had changed.

Except that her love was alive.

And Angus had said she was loved in return.

There was nothng else to do. She stepped forward.

Hamish took her hand.

Her hand...

This wasn't what she wanted. It wasn't what she had half hoped for—half expected. She wanted—quite desperately—to be seized, crushed against his good shoulder and kissed.

Solidly kissed.

Instead of which, she was being held by the hand and Hamish's twinkling smile was suddenly uncertain.

'Lilly, you saved my life,' he said softly. 'And Steven's.'

'It was my. . .my pleasure.' It was a stupid thing to say, but she could think of nothing else.

'The nurses here have been updating me on all the gossip,' Hamish smiled, without releasing her hand. 'I gather Steven's eating breakfast, too, and telling everyone within earshot what happened.'

'He knows enough for the police to prosecute Owen?'

'He sure does. Not that it's needed now. Oswald will have enough charges against him to keep him behind bars for a very long time.'

'S-so what happened?' This was a safe subject. Safe when the very air round them seemed charged with something that Lilly couldn't begin to define. The link between their hands seemed almost to burn but Hamish made no move to release her.

Hamish hesitated. Like Lilly, he too seemed to sense the tension—and finally ignored it enough to stay on this nice safe subject.

'It seems Claire went outside with Owen Oswald at the party,' Hamish told her. Only his eyes, carefully watching Lilly's face, betrayed his knowledge of her tension.

'Steven was annoyed,' he continued. 'He went outside, hid in the shadows and did a bit of eavesdropping. What he heard horrified him. It seems Owen talked Claire into taking LSD because people would think she was a baby if she wasn't game to try what everyone else was trying—as if they were.

'Steven started listening after she'd taken the stuff but just in time to hear Owen threatening dreadful things to Claire's family if she ever revealed her supplier. The boy didn't know what the side-effects would be, but when Claire was so ill the next day he just went berserk and made his own threats. To Owen.'

'And was nearly killed for his pains.' Lilly nodded. 'I hope Claire's grateful.'

'She's giving a statement to the police this morning,' Hamish told her. 'See, I have my ear to all the hospital gossip already. I gather when Claire found out what Owen had done to Steven she broke down and told the police everything.'

'I'm glad,' Lilly said simply.

'So am I.' Hamish looked down at their linked hands. 'And...and very grateful, Lilly.' He looked up at her and saw her face was white and drawn. The tension was stretching to breaking point. 'Don't look like that, Lilly,' he said gently, withdrawing his hand. 'I'm not about to put any more pressure on you. I've told you before, I'm not the bastard you think me.'

'Hamish, don't,' Lilly managed, in a voice that seemed strained even to her ears. 'I never thought you were a bastard.'

Silence.

Now or never, she told herself frantically. Now!

'Hamish, it's true,' Lilly said gently. And somehow the words were there. Somehow the words came out all by themselves. 'I swear I never thought that. How... how can I think the man I love with all my heart is a lying toad? When I love you so much, how...how can I believe that?'

The silence changed.

The tension was at breaking point and beyond. Out in the corridor a ward attendant was clearing trays but the clattering didn't break the breathless hush in the room.

Let the ward's maid please not come near here yet, Lilly prayed silently. Please...

'You're saying you love me?' he said slowly. His face was absolutely still.

'I always have,' Lilly said simply. 'Hamish, I fell in love with you five long years ago and I've never stopped loving you. Not for a minute. Even when I thought you were married. I've always loved you, and I always will.' She looked down at her empty hands and winced.

'You. . .you can do with that what you want. I decided last night that I should tell you.' She managed to tilt her chin and look at him. 'And then you went and got yourself shot and I couldn't.'

There seemed nothing left to say. Lilly stepped back from the bed. She felt more alone at this moment than she had ever felt in her life. She had done all she could. She was putting her trust in Angus McVie's crazy statement—that Hamish loved her.

Angus wanted a bridal remedy. This was his last chance to have one.

'Lilly.'

Hamish's voice was a low growl.

'Y-yes.' She didn't look up. She couldn't.

'You were going to tell me this last night.'

'Yes.'

'Why?'

'I. . . Angus told me that you loved me,' she said simply. 'He knows, you see. He knows I love you.'

'Why the hell are you standing so damned far away from the bed?'

'I. . .' Lilly gasped as Hamish threw back the covers. 'Hamish, don't you dare. You can't. For heaven's sake, you're still hooked up to a drip.'

'Then get back here this instant or I'll come and fetch you, drip and all.'

'But. . .'

'Don't *but* me, girl!' Hamish's voice was practically a shout. 'How dare you say you love me and then step back from the bed when. . .? Dammit, I'm weak as a kitten. Lilly, get back here. Please. . .' He gave a strangled moan. 'The girl I love says she loves me and I can't even reach her. *Lilly, get back here or I'll get up and fetch you and be damned with the consequences.*'

The girl I love. . .

'Hamish. . .' Lilly didn't move. She spread her hands helplessly and looked down at him. 'Hamish. . .'

'Please, Lilly. . .' It was a groan of despair. Hamish

reached forward and if Lilly hadn't moved, in another second he would have fallen sideways.

As it was, she caught him—and was gripped hard for her pains. So hard that it hurt.

'Lilly, why didn't you agree to marry me when I asked you?' He held her at arm's length so that he could see her face, but his grip was like steel.

'Hamish, you'll make yourself start bleeding again. For heaven's sake, you'll hurt your shoulder. You should be still.'

'So tell me fast.'

'I didn't. . .' She took a deep breath. 'I didn't think you loved me. I thought. . .I just thought you'd decided it was. . .it was the sensible thing to do.'

This time the silence was loaded.

'You didn't think I loved you?' he managed at last in the voice of a man goaded beyond endurance.

'N-no.'

'Lilly. . .'

'Y-yes?'

'Bend over.'

'Why?'

'Because I'm asking you to,' he said softly. 'I'm a dangerously ill man, Lilly Inger, and a good doctor knows a dangerously ill patient has to be humoured at all costs. So bend!'

And Lilly looked down at those dangerous, triumphant, laughing eyes and she knew just what she had to do.

She bent.

'Let's get one thing straight right now,' Hamish said softly, as his good arm came round her shoulder in a grip that was possessive and brooked no argument. His eyes were inches from hers, his mouth so close they were almost touching.

'I am not in the habit of marrying for convenience. I made one disastrous marriage when I was twenty years old and I'm not about to make another. If I marry again,

I marry for keeps. And the only girl I'd consider being married to for the rest of my life is in my arms—my arm—right now.'

'But. . .'

'Shut up, love,' he said kindly. 'I haven't finished. I love you more than life itself, Lilly Inger. For now and for ever. For as long as we both shall live.'

His eyes searched hers. 'Lilly, it's the truth. If I've never said the words ''I love you'' it's not because I haven't thought them. Lilly, I didn't say them because I thought it was unfair. Burdening you with emotion I could hardly cope with myself.

'Firstly I was still married, Lilly, no matter how much of a mockery that marriage was. How could I tie you to me so tightly? I thought. . .I remember thinking I'd arrange the divorce and then. . .then you wouldn't have been able to stop the declarations. Only it didn't happen.

'And these last few weeks it seemed just as unfair to bind you to me when you didn't want. . .you didn't seem to want anything to do with me. But, Lilly, all I've ever wanted to do for five long years is to bind you to me so tightly you'll never want to leave. With love, Lilly. With love.'

And his good hand came up to clasp the back of her head and hold her close.

The silence went on and on.

For a long, long moment their eyes locked, and the vows that were made in that silent moment were vows that would last for ever.

And then Hamish Campbell's lips met hers and there was still no need for words.

Two hearts joined to become one.

For ever.

EPILOGUE

IT WAS a glorious day for a wedding.

The breeze sweeping the island was laden with the scent of eucalypts and the island's tiny chapel was packed to bursting. Most of Nooluk had turned out for this magic wedding of two of the island's three doctors.

For Hamish, this was a second wedding. At thirty-five, Dr Hamish Campbell was one of the most popular men on the island, his caring smile and other, more masculine attributes tempting the island's younger women—and some not so young—to insist that sore throats should be seen almost as soon as they tickled.

And Lilly—gentle, lovely Lilly with her delicious chuckle that surfaced at a moment's notice and her cloud of burnished curls—seemed every man's dream. A fairy-tale bride. . .

The hour had come. Only the tinkling of bellbirds in the branches high above the church broke the stillness. The church doors drew apart and every head turned to see.

Then the bellbirds were drowned out by the pure, triumphant notes of the 'Trumpet Voluntary'. Every man, woman and child drew in their breaths at the vision floating down the aisle—at Lilly moving slowly, mistily down the aisle toward her beloved Hamish.

Before her, proudly bearing two rings on a white velvet cushion, was Lilly's small son. Four-year-old Davey was perhaps the proudest person in church. He walked solemnly, carefully down the aisle before his mother's cloud of lace and satin, and finally stepped aside to take the hand of the man who'd escorted Lilly down the aisle.

The man whose hand he took was Dr Angus McVie,

the island's third doctor. White-haired and halfway into his seventies, Angus smiled down at Davey—his soon-to-be great-nephew-by-marriage—and his wrinkled hand squeezed the trusting fingers of the child.

This was the answer to both their needs, the squeeze said. The joining of both their loved ones. . .

And then Angus McVie and four-year-old Davey stood silently together, man and child, to see Lilly and Hamish become one.

GET 4 BOOKS
AND A MYSTERY GIFT

Return this coupon and we'll send you 4 Medical Romance™ novels and a mystery gift absolutely FREE! We'll even pay the postage and packing for you.

We're making you this offer to introduce you to the benefits of Reader Service: FREE home delivery of brand-new Medical Romance novels, at least a month before they are available in the shops, FREE gifts and a monthly Newsletter packed with information.

Accepting these FREE books and gift places you under no obligation to buy, you may cancel at any time, even after receiving just your free shipment. Simply complete the coupon below and send it to:

MILLS & BOON® READER SERVICE, FREEPOST, CROYDON, SURREY, CR9 3WZ.

No stamp needed

Yes, please send me 4 free Medical Romance novels and a mystery gift. I understand that unless you hear from me, I will receive 4 superb new titles every month for just £2.10* each, postage and packing free. I am under no obligation to purchase any books and I may cancel or suspend my subscription at any time, but the free books and gift will be mine to keep in any case. (I am over 18 years of age)

M6LE

Ms/Mrs/Miss/Mr _____

Address _____

_____

_____ Postcode _____

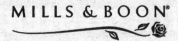

MILLS & BOON®

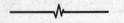 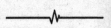

Books for enjoyment this month...

RESPONDING TO TREATMENT	Abigail Gordon
BRIDAL REMEDY	Marion Lennox
A WISH FOR CHRISTMAS	Josie Metcalfe
WINGS OF DUTY	Meredith Webber

Treats in store!

Watch next month for these absorbing stories...

TAKE A CHANCE ON LOVE	Jean Evans
PARTNERS IN LOVE	Maggie Kingsley
DRASTIC MEASURES	Laura MacDonald
PERFECT PARTNERS	Carol Wood